THE PET FINDERS CLUB

THE PET FINDERS CLUB

1: Come Back Buddy

2: Max is Missing

3: Looking for Lola

4: Rescuing Raisin

5: The Dog with No Name

6: Searching for Sunshine

7: Disappearing Desert Kittens

8: Dachshund in Danger

9: Runaway Rascal

10: Help Honey

THE PET FINDERS CLUB

Dachshund in Danger

BEN M. BAGLIO

*Hodder
Children's
Books*

A division of Hachette Children's Books

Special thanks to Liss Norton

First published in the USA in 2005 by Scholastic Inc

First published in Great Britain in 2008
by Hodder Children's Books

ISBN-13: 978 0 340 93137 0

Typeset in Weiss by Avon DataSet Ltd,
Bidford on Avon, Warwickshire

Printed and bound in Great Britain by
CPI Bookmarque, Croydon, CR0 4TD

The paper and board used in this paperback by Hodder Children's
Books are natural recyclable products made from wood grown in
sustainable forests. The manufacturing processes conform to the
environmental regulations of the country of origin.

Hodder Children's Books
a division of Hachette Children's Books
338 Euston Road, London NW1 3BH
An Hachette Livre UK Company

Chapter One

Andi Talbot turned up her collar against the January sleet and tried to smile at her friend, Natalie Lewis. "I love taking Buddy out, but I won't be sorry to get inside today. It's freezing!"

Natalie tucked the ends of her purple scarf into her padded jacket. "Totally!" she agreed, shivering.

Andi's cute tan-and-white Jack Russell terrier raced up when he heard his name. He jumped up, his mouth open in a wide doggy grin, then charged away across the park. Natalie's black Labrador, Jet, galloped after him, his ears streaming backwards.

"I don't want to worry you, Nat," Andi began, "but I think Jet's on a collision course with that puddle." She pointed to a deep patch of churned-up mud, too wide for Jet to jump.

"Jet, no!" Natalie yelled.

To Andi's relief, Buddy dodged the patch of mud

and sat down on the other side with his tongue hanging out. Unfortunately, Jet didn't follow. He bounded straight into the puddle, splashing mud all over his shiny black coat.

"Oh no," Natalie moaned. "Come here, Jet. And sit!"

Jet sat down in the puddle.

"I didn't mean sit *there*. I meant come *out* and sit down." Natalie sighed, then began to giggle.

Andi started laughing, too. "It's a good thing we're on the way to his Obedience class," she said. "Now that Jet's learned 'sit', perhaps he can learn 'come'."

Natalie rolled her eyes. "I wish." She patted her knees. "Come on, Jet. Get out of there."

Jet trotted to her and wagged his tail against her jeans, smearing them with mud. "You're totally impossible," Natalie said. She ruffled his ears and gave him a dog treat. "Goodness knows what Fisher's going to say when he sees you."

"He won't mind," Andi said. Fisher Pearce, the local RSPCA vet, ran the dog-training classes. "He's mad about dogs." She glanced at Jet and grinned. "Even muddy ones."

The dog-training classes were held in a spacious room behind the RSPCA centre. Through the brightly-lit windows, Andi and Natalie could see people milling about inside with their dogs. Andi felt a tingle of excitement. This was her first visit to Natalie's class, and she couldn't wait to meet all the dogs and their owners. "There's Gemma," Natalie said, pointing to a dark-haired girl aged about fourteen. A gorgeous chestnut-and-white cocker spaniel was bouncing round her ankles. "And that's Crumble," Natalie added. "You'll love him."

They pushed the door open and went into a narrow entrance hall. "I'll get some paper towels so we can try to clean Jet up," Andi said. She fetched some from the toilets, and she and Natalie started rubbing his thick black fur. Jet licked Natalie's face. "He thinks you're dirty, too," Andi joked.

A broad-shouldered man wearing faded denim jeans arrived, leading a very lively black-and-white spotted crossbreed puppy. Andi guessed it had some Dalmatian in its ancestry.

"Evening, Natalie," the man said.

"Hello, Mr Taylor! How's Dapple getting on?"

"Not too bad. He's down to two pairs of trainers a day now. I keep telling him I won't buy any more once he's chewed through every pair I own! And it looks as though Jet's had a fun walk!" He grinned. "Hello there," he said to Andi. "Are you starting Obedience lessons today?"

"No. Buddy and I are just watching," Andi replied. She took a break from dabbing at Jet's fur to pat Dapple. The adorable puppy twisted his head to lick her hand.

"This is my friend, Andi," Natalie said.

"Well, I hope you enjoy the lesson, Andi." Mr Taylor stroked Buddy's head before going through the swing doors that led into the main room.

The door opened again and a tan-and-black German Shepherd bounded in, tugging a tiny woman behind him. "Wait, Prince!" she called. "Oh hello, Natalie." The woman yanked on Prince's lead, but he dragged her straight past them without stopping.

"Hello, Jan," Natalie called after her. She shook her head. "Prince hasn't got the hang of walking to heel yet." She straightened up, wiping her hands on her muddy jeans. "Come on, Jet. You're as clean as we're going to get you."

Andi and Natalie threw away the muddy paper towels and went into the RSPCA hall. Fisher Pearce was on the other side of the room, bending down to make a fuss of a plump and hairy Pekingese. "See you later, Chester." He ruffled the little dog's fur, then came to greet Natalie and Andi. "Hello, you two. Are you and Buddy joining in, Andi?"

"No. Just watching."

"Right you are. You can keep Christine company."

Christine Wilson, the owner of the local pet shop, Paws for Thought, was sitting at the far end of the room. She waved to Andi and patted the empty seat beside her. "Come and sit with me," she called.

"Thanks! I'll be there in a mo."

Suddenly, a Jack Russell puppy came scampering into the hall on an extending lead held by a woman about the same age as Andi's mum.

Andi couldn't resist going over to say hello. "He's adorable," she said, holding out her hand so the pup could sniff her.

"I know!" his owner agreed. "And so is your dog. Jack Russells are lovely, aren't they?"

"They are," Andi said eagerly. She patted the puppy with one hand and stroked Buddy with the other so he wouldn't feel left out. The puppy's coat felt much softer than Buddy's because he hadn't lost all of his baby fluff yet.

Natalie joined them. "Hello, Mrs Price. This is my friend, Andi. She's come to watch the lesson." She bent down to stroke the puppy. "Hello, Louis. How are you?"

Louis licked her fingers, then stretched up to touch noses with Buddy.

"OK, everyone," said Fisher, raising his voice above the chatter. "Let's get started."

"See you later, Nat," Andi said. "Good luck." She clipped on Buddy's lead and took him over to the row of chairs. "Hello, Christine."

"Hello there. How's pet-finding? Have you got any cases on the go?"

"No, not at the moment." Andi, Natalie and their friend Tristan Saunders had formed the Pet Finders Club soon after Andi moved to Aldcliffe, a suburb of Lancaster, from Texas in America. They'd already found lots of pets, including a pony and some reptiles that had been stolen from Christine's shop. "Nobody's told *you* about any lost pets, have they?" Andi asked hopefully. She'd love to have another case to investigate.

"No. But don't worry – if they do, I'll give them one of your flyers. I've got a whole stack of them on the counter. Tristan is always topping it up."

Tristan's mum was Christine's cousin, and he often helped out at the shop.

"We're going to learn the sit-and-stay command today," Fisher announced from the middle of the room. "First, get your dogs to sit."

Andi was pleased when Jet sat straight away on Natalie's command. "He's definitely getting better," she whispered to Christine.

She nodded. "Fisher is a great teacher."

Unfortunately Prince, the German Shepherd, wasn't in the mood for lessons. He jumped about on the end of his lead and it took all Jan's strength to keep him in one place. "Sit!" she shouted. At once all the dogs, including Buddy, sat down.

Everyone laughed – except for Jan. She blushed scarlet.

"Don't forget to give Prince a treat, Jan," Fisher reminded her. "It may have taken him a while, but he sat down in the end and he needs to be rewarded for it. Now," he went on, "I want you to tell your dogs to stay, then move a couple of steps away."

The Pekingese was the only dog to stay put when his owner, a huge man with a bushy beard, walked away. "Chester probably can't see what's going on from under all that hair," Andi whispered.

Christine grinned. "Do you think his owner should swap dogs with the woman with the German Shepherd?" she joked.

In spite of the puddle incident on the way to the lesson, Jet was doing really well. Andi caught Natalie's eye and gave her a thumbs-up.

There was a draught around Andi's feet as the door at the end of the room opened. A brown-haired man aged about thirty came in and tiptoed down to the chairs. A stunning chocolate-coloured collie trotted beside him on tiny, delicate paws.

The collie's owner sat down next to Andi. "Hello, are you here for the Musical Freestyling?"

Andi frowned. "No, but it sounds interesting. What is it?"

The man stretched his long legs in front of him and grinned. "I suppose you could call it dancing for dogs."

Andi was intrigued. *"Dancing for dogs?"*

"That's right. Just think of doing all the basic Obedience movements, but with a musical soundtrack. The dogs love it."

Andi clicked her fingers and the collie came and sat beside her. She ran her fingers through the dog's thick fur. "Brown's a really unusual colour for a collie, isn't it?"

"Yes. It's pretty though, don't you think?" the man said proudly.

"She's gorgeous," Andi agreed. "What's her name?"

"Whisper. And I'm Shaun Carter."

"I'm Andi Talbot and this is Buddy." Andi bent down to smooth Bud's fur in case he was feeling left out. "I'm a member of the Pet Finders Club. You might have heard of us?"

Shaun's hazel eyes lit up. "I've seen your posters in the high street. I think it's great what you do. You must really love animals."

Andi nodded and gave Buddy a hug.

"Have you got time to watch the Freestyling class?" Shaun went on. "I think you'd really like it."

"I'd love to!" said Andi. "Will your teacher mind having an audience?"

"I'm sure she won't, but let's ask her. That's Chloe coming in now." He stood up and waved to a tall young woman who had just slipped through the swing doors.

Andi thought Chloe didn't look much like a dog-obedience teacher. Her short, spiky hair was dyed black, and she was wearing a black denim skirt with rainbow-coloured leggings underneath. A rather haughty-looking cream Pomeranian padded beside her. Chloe crept down the hall towards them, the dog's claws clicking on the floor. "Hi, Shaun. Hi, Whisper."

"This is Andi Talbot," Shaun said quietly. "Is it OK if she watches our lesson?"

"Of course." Chloe smiled. "The more, the merrier."

"Thanks." Andi watched as more owners and dogs crowded into the hall. The Freestyling class looked very popular. "I don't suppose you've got any spaces in the class, have you?"

"I've got room for two more this term." Chloe raised her eyebrows. "Why, are you interested?"

"I think so. It sounds like a really good idea. And I'm sure my friend Natalie would like to join, too. That's her over there with the black Labrador."

"Why don't you both watch this week and see how you feel when you know what we do?" Chloe suggested.

Andi beamed at her. "We'll do that, thanks."

"That's all for today," Fisher called. "Thanks for coming. And keep practising."

Natalie raced over to Andi. "Jet did brilliantly, didn't he?"

"Yes, a big improvement! Listen, Nat, there's a dance class for dogs next. Shall we stay and watch?"

"A dog dance class? Sounds amazing."

Fisher came over. "Would you like to go out to eat, Christine? There's a new Italian place just opened round the corner."

Christine smiled up at him. "Italian! My favourite!"

As they headed for the door, Natalie caught Andi's eye and winked. Andi sighed inwardly. Natalie saw something romantic in just about everything!

Chloe went into the centre of the room and smiled at the expectant circle of dogs and owners. "Hello, everyone. We'll start a new step today, called 'backing'. First we'll have you moving forwards while your dogs go backwards, then we'll try both of you

11

backing away from each other at the same time. Purdy and I will demonstrate." She raised her right hand and the Pomeranian pricked up her ears.

Chloe crooked her finger and took a step forwards. Purdy backed away, stepping in time with her owner.

"Now you try. You can use any signal – a flat hand, flicking your fingers, anything you like really – but it must always be the same one. And you've got to keep that signal going until you want your dog to stop. We'll try it first without music."

Andi watched Shaun and Whisper closely. Shaun raised his hand, then took one pace towards Whisper. The collie stepped back, her gaze fixed on Shaun's hand. Shaun kept going forwards and after a couple of moments, Whisper seemed to understand what he wanted and backed in time with his steps. Andi was spellbound.

As though he could sense what she was thinking, Buddy leant against her leg. "We'll be doing this soon, Bud," Andi told him, rubbing his chest.

"Well done, everyone," Chloe said. "Now let's try it to music." She pointed a remote control at a portable stereo system and lively rock music began to play.

Shaun and Whisper moved perfectly in time to the music and when Shaun jauntily swung his hips, Whisper did the same. Shaun saw Andi watching and smiled.

12

"That's fantastic!" Andi whispered to Natalie.

"Now try the same thing facing away from your dog," Chloe instructed the class. "You just need to give the same signal behind your back. And you might like to add in some of the pivot turns we practised last week."

Halfway through the next track, an alarm beeped on Shaun's mobile.

"Sorry, Chloe, I've got to go," he called. "It's my turn to look after the babies." Clicking his fingers, he hurried towards the door. Whisper followed as though she was glued to his heel.

"How many babies has Shaun got?" Natalie wondered. "Twins? Or triplets?"

"Six," Chloe said with a smile, overhearing her.

"Six?" Andi gasped.

Chloe laughed. "Don't worry, they're not human babies. Shaun and his wife breed miniature long-haired dachshunds. One of their champions, Tooey, had puppies two weeks ago."

Natalie looked puzzled. "He's going home to look after puppies? Doesn't their mum do that?"

"The Carters are devoted to their dogs," Chloe explained. "They never leave new mums alone for the first few weeks."

Andi exchanged a glance with Natalie. That was

the kind of pet owner they approved of! She settled down happily to watch the rest of the class.

Andi stuck her head round the living-room door. "Hello, Mum. Can I check my emails please?"

"Of course you can, darling."

Andi ran up to the study with Buddy at her heels and logged on to the Internet. "Yes!" she exclaimed, punching the air. There was an email from Nina Nelson, who lived in Tucson, Arizona, at the Santa Rosa Crafts shop. Andi had helped Nina find three semi-feral kittens while she'd been staying with her dad in America at New Year.

Hi, Andi. Things are great here. The kittens are growing soooo fast. Dezba is turning out to be a champion curtain-climber! You can guess how much Granddad appreciates her talent. Nascha and Yas have their work cut out to keep up with their big sister. You know how I said I'd have to let the kittens go if they wanted to live feral like their mum? Well, I have some *really* great news: whenever I put them outside, they keep coming back in! It looks like they want to live here for good – and even better, Granddad says they can stay!

Andi hugged Buddy, picturing the three adorable kittens playing all over the busy shop. She knew how much being able to keep the kittens would mean to Nina. And best of all, as far as Andi was concerned, it meant she'd be able to see Dezba, Nascha and Yas next time she visited her dad. "This is brilliant news, Buddy!"

She quickly typed an email with her congratulations, and told Nina all about the Musical Freestyling class she'd watched. Andi was really glad Shaun had invited her to stay and watch the class. It looked like great fun! She couldn't wait to try out the moves with Buddy next week. He was always surprising her with how clever he was, and how quick at picking up new things. Perhaps he'd be a champion dancing dog, just like Whisper!

Chapter Two

Andi was a few minutes late arriving at school next morning – Buddy had got wet on their walk after breakfast, and she'd wanted to make sure he was completely dry before she left – so she hurried straight to her classroom. She stopped in the doorway, wincing at the amount of noise her classmates were making while they waited for Mr Dixon, their teacher, to arrive.

Andi glanced at the hamster cage in the corner of the classroom. She wondered how the newest addition to the class was handling the din. They'd only had Cinnamon for two weeks and Andi hoped the little hamster wasn't trying to sleep!

She went over and peered into the cage. It had two floors linked by a metal ladder. On the lower floor were an exercise wheel and a little plastic house with shredded paper spilling out of the doorway. A bowl of nuts and seeds stood beside it and a water bottle was fastened to the bars.

There was no sign of Cinnamon, but Andi knew that hamsters sometimes buried themselves in order to feel safe and warm. She looked more closely and noticed that some of the shredded paper was twitching, so she guessed he was asleep in his little house. Andi didn't want to disturb him so she headed for her seat.

As she squeezed past one of the other tables, Tanya McLennan flung out her arms, sending Andi's rucksack flying.

"Oops! Sorry, Andi." Tanya, a pretty girl with a small turned-up nose, picked up the bag and handed it back. "I was just trying to demonstrate the size of the teddy bear I'm going to buy for Marie's birthday." Her green eyes sparkled with excitement.

Andi knew Tanya's little sister had been in hospital recently to have an operation on her leg. "How is Marie?" she asked.

"She's much better now," Tanya said. Some of the sparkle went out of her eyes, showing how worried she'd been. "The doctor said she can go back to school after her birthday. She's mad about animals so she'll love this bear."

"It sounds great," Andi said.

She had just sat down when the door swung open and Mr Dixon backed into the room carrying two enormous white boxes. "OK, everybody, let's settle down," he said, setting the boxes on his desk.

Across the table from Andi, her friend Chen half stood up to get a better look at the white boxes. "What do you think he's got there?"

Andi could see more clearly from her seat. "There's something written on the side." She craned her neck. "Treetops Hotel, Aldcliffe," she read out loud. She frowned. "What would a hotel send to a school?" All she could think of were clean towels, or those miniature soaps her mum collected for her when she went away on business.

"I bet Mr Dixon's borrowed the boxes for something boring, like extra exercise books," sighed Howard, who sat next to Chen.

"That's enough chatter," said Mr Dixon. "We'll take the register, then I've got some good news for you."

"Fingers crossed we won't have to do any homework this week," whispered Chen.

"Or maths is cancelled," joked Larissa, who sat between Howard and Andi.

As soon as the register had been taken, Mr Dixon lifted the lid on one of the white boxes. "I know you're all dying to know what's in here . . ." There was more writing on the lid but it was upside down and written in swirly writing. Andi squinted, trying to work out what it said.

"Lance Sinden, Baking Specialist," she read.

"Do you think Mr Dixon's brought us something to eat?" Howard whispered.

"It *is* something to eat, Howard," said Mr Dixon, who could hear like a bat when people were talking at the back of the class, "but it might not be for you. I might decide to eat all of these cakes myself." His eyes twinkled. "In fact, I might just take them down to the staff room. Teaching's a tiring job and we need the occasional treat to keep our strength up."

The class laughed. Everyone knew he was joking.

"Lance Sinden, who used to go to this school, is the new pastry chef at the Treetops Hotel," Mr Dixon explained, as if he had decided not to keep them in suspense any longer, "so he's arranged for the hotel to send every child a sample of his handiwork – though why they think you deserve them, I can't imagine!"

"What kind of cakes are they?" Chen called.

Mr Dixon began to hand round the boxes. "Chocolate muffins and strawberry tarts."

Andi chose a strawberry tart. It was delicious, with soft crumbly pastry and just the right amount of fruity filling. "Yum," she said, licking her fingers. "I wish we could have one of these every morning!"

"Me, too," Larissa agreed.

Andi saw Natalie tucking into a chocolate muffin. There were a few crumbs clinging to her cheek. Andi tried to catch her eye, but Nat was too busy eating to notice her frantic signal.

"OK, while you're eating, you also need to listen. Firstly, we'll be making a big thank you card to send to Mr Sinden this afternoon. Secondly, while I've got your attention, I want to tell you more about this term's topic. As you know, we're linking everything to the theme of pets," Mr Dixon said. "So not just science or geography, but maths, English and art, too."

"Maths?" Kelly queried. "How can maths fit into a pet topic?"

Mr Dixon grinned. "With a little imagination, you'll find numbers everywhere you look! You can calculate the amount of food your pet eats in a week, a month, or a year. Or work out how far a hamster walks on a wheel. Or how far we walk our dogs . . ."

"I'm going to do my project on Buddy," Andi told Larissa in a low voice.

"You're really lucky having a dog," Howard interrupted, "but I haven't got any pets. What am I going to do my project about?"

"I'm going to use my aunt's cat," Larissa said. "Is there someone else in your family with a pet, Howard?"

Howard looked glum. "No."

"Anyone who doesn't have a pet," Mr Dixon went on, as though he'd overheard, "can do their project on Cinnamon."

"Oh great!" Howard moodily flicked his pencil across the table. "A project about a weedy little hamster!"

"He's not weedy," protested Kelly, who sat opposite Larissa. "I haven't got a pet either and I'm going to *love* studying Cinnamon. Why don't we do our project together?" She pulled some books out of her rucksack. "I've been reading up about hamsters." Howard looked a bit startled when Kelly stacked the books in front of him.

"Howard, will you give out the science sheets, please?" Mr Dixon called.

Andi read through the questions on the sheet. The first one was: *What does your pet eat?* With Buddy, that was pretty much everything! Leftover pizza, apple cores, sandwich crusts . . .

Howard finished giving out the worksheets and slumped down in his chair again. "Why can't I have a Rottweiler or something?" he complained.

"Come over to Cinnamon's cage," said Kelly.

'We can have a look at his food and see exactly what's in it."

"Hamsters are *boring*," Howard insisted, sliding lower in his chair.

"Come on." Kelly grabbed his arm and dragged him to his feet. "Give us a hand here, Andi."

Trying not to giggle, Andi helped Kelly march Howard to the hamster cage. Larissa came too, pushing him from behind.

Cinnamon was out of bed now. Andi admired the pretty tan blotches on his snow-white fur, the exact colour of the warm orange spice he was named after. He was busy rearranging the wood chippings that covered the cage floor.

"Hello, boy," Kelly said, letting go of Howard and bending down to look into the cage.

Cinnamon sat up on his hind legs and looked at her, his whiskers twitching.

Larissa pushed her finger through the bars of Cinnamon's cage. "Here, Cinnamon."

The hamster came to the bars and sniffed her finger, then gave it a sharp nip.

"Ow!" Larissa yelped, yanking her hand back.

Cinnamon leapt away from the bars as though he'd been stung and scurried into his house.

"Is Cinnamon all right?" Kelly gasped.

Andi peered through the doorway. "Yes, he's fine. He's nibbling a seed."

"What about me?" Larissa protested.

"Have you been touching any fruit?" Kelly asked, examining her friend's finger.

Larissa looked baffled. "Umm . . . Only my apple. I put it in my bag just before I left home this morning."

Kelly darted back to her table and returned with a book. She turned to a page that was marked with a slip of yellow paper. "It says here that hamsters have bad eyesight so they use their sense of smell to find out what things are."

"So Cinnamon thought Larissa's finger was a slice of apple?" Howard said. His face brightened. "Hey, maybe hamsters aren't so boring after all!"

The rest of the week flew by. While Andi was busy working on her Buddy project, Howard got more and more excited about studying Cinnamon. Every morning, he bombarded Andi with the latest facts he had learnt about hamsters. He had discovered that they came from desert areas and that they liked a sand bath to roll in, like chinchillas. Howard had decided to buy some chinchilla sand for Cinnamon from Paws for Thought.

"But people ought to learn how to handle him

properly," he added seriously, his eyebrows knitting together in a frown. "I've seen loads of people holding him too tight. Hamsters are delicate animals and it's easy to squash them."

"I suppose we're all still learning about hamsters," Andi said, distracted by a sum she was doing about how far she walked Buddy in a month.

"I'm going to speak to Mr Dixon about it," Howard announced. "It's not fair to Cinnamon if people don't pick him up carefully. In fact, there are some people in this class who don't deserve to have a hamster at all."

On Monday evening, Andi and Buddy stopped at Tristan's house on their way to their Musical Freestyling lesson. "Come in," he said, opening the door. "I've just got to feed Lucy." He grabbed a tin of cat food and forked some into her bowl. "Lucy," he called, setting the bowl down on her mat in the corner of the kitchen.

"Come on," Andi said. "I don't want to be late for my first lesson."

"Yeah, almost ready. Lucy! Dinner!"

There was no sign of his pretty tabby cat. "Hang on, I'll see if she's upstairs." Tristan raced up the stairs.

Andi heard him going from room to room, calling. "Tris!" she yelled.

Tristan ran down again. "She must be out in the garden." He darted to the back door and flung it open. "Lucy! Dinner!"

"I'll go without you," Andi warned.

"There she is!" Lucy was sitting on a raised wooden deck, half hidden behind a huge flowerpot. "Come on, girl. Aren't you cold sitting out here?"

Lucy stood up and stretched before padding calmly towards Tristan. He scooped her up, carried her into the house and set her down by her bowl. "I'm ready now," he said, washing his hands.

"About time." Andi glanced at her watch. The class was due to start in ten minutes. "We'll have to run."

As they sprinted across the car park outside the RSPCA centre, Andi saw Shaun arriving with Whisper. "Hello, Shaun," she called. "How are the babies?"

Beside her, Tristan looked puzzled, but Shaun grinned. "They're great, actually. Thank you for asking."

Then, taking pity on Tristan's baffled expression, Andi explained what the "babies" were.

"I bet miniature dachshund puppies are really cute," he said. "I've never seen one before."

"That's easily fixed," said Shaun. "Would you two and Natalie like to come and see them sometime?"

"Yes, please!" Andi whooped.

"If it's OK with your parents, you can come

whenever you like." Shaun wrote down his address and gave it to Andi.

"Could we come tomorrow after school?" Tristan asked hopefully.

"That sounds perfect," Shaun replied.

"Brilliant!" Andi said, as they went into the hall.

They arrived just as the Basic Obedience class ended. "Jet's done really well today, Natalie," Fisher Pearce was saying.

The Labrador barked and wagged his tail, as if he was glad Fisher had noticed.

Chloe arrived and Andi found a space near Natalie to work in. "This is going to be great," she said excitedly. Tristan gave them a thumbs-up from the chairs at the end of the room.

"Hello, everyone," said Chloe. "Welcome to Andi and Buddy, and Natalie and Jet, our newest students." Everyone smiled warmly at the two girls. Chloe continued, "We're going to practise backing again today."

After a bit of instruction from Chloe, Andi raised her hand and crooked her finger as she'd seen Chloe do in the previous class. Buddy jumped up to lick her hand.

"No, Bud," Andi said. "That's the signal for backing. You have to walk away from me." She took a step

27

forwards and Buddy jumped up again, his tail wagging.

Andi laughed. "Let's watch Whisper for a bit," she said.

Buddy sat beside her and they watched Whisper back across the hall, keeping in time with Shaun's steps.

"That's how it's done, Bud." Andi faced Buddy again and made the backing signal.

Buddy glanced at Whisper, then stepped back.

"Brilliant!" Andi exclaimed. She stepped forward and Buddy took another pace back. He kept looking across at Whisper, as if he wanted to make sure he was doing it properly.

"Buddy's a natural," Shaun praised. "He seems to have a real feel for the beat."

Andi beamed. "Thanks! I think he's learnt from watching Whisper."

At the end of the class, Andi and Natalie hurried over to speak to Tristan. "What did you think?" Andi demanded.

Tristan shrugged. "Hmm, not bad. Maybe I should bring Lucy next week. She's got amazing musical taste. Every time my mum plays one of her CDs, Lucy runs out of the room!"

Andi laughed.

"Bye," called Shaun. "See you tomorrow."

"What did he mean?" said Natalie.

"He's invited us to see Tooey's puppies," Andi explained.

"Fantastic!" Natalie exclaimed. "We're meeting so many new dogs, I'm starting to feel like I might grow fur and a tail!"

Chapter Three

Andi's mum offered to go with the Pet Finders to visit the miniature dachshunds, so she picked them up straight after school and drove them to Shaun Carter's house. A sports car was parked on the driveway and there was a bird table loaded with food near the front door. A few birds were feeding, but they flew away as the Pet Finders approached.

"I hope they come back," Tristan said. "Birds need plenty of food at this time of year to keep warm."

"Six puppies," Natalie breathed as she rang the doorbell. "I can't wait to see them."

"Me neither," Andi agreed. She'd been thinking about them all day at school, and had got into trouble twice for not paying attention.

Mrs Talbot laughed. "I remember all the things Buddy got up to when he was a puppy. Imagine having six little bundles of mischief!"

Shaun Carter opened the door with Whisper at his heels. "Come in! I'm glad you could make it." Andi introduced her mum and Mrs Talbot shook hands with Shaun. Then he led them into a spacious living room lined with windows reaching from floor to ceiling. A library of dog books filled a bookcase on the far side of the room, and the mantelpiece was crammed with photos of miniature dachshund puppies.

"Eleanor, my wife, isn't here, so it's just me and Whisper pup-watching this afternoon," Shaun explained. Tooey and her pups were lying in a woven basket in a patch of winter sunlight. A bowl of water stood nearby.

Tooey was an adorable cylinder of silky chocolate and black hair, with long floppy ears edged with a velvety soft fringe. She lifted her head as the Pet Finders came in, and her plumy cocoa-coloured tail began to wag. Six puppies, looking like tiny balls of fluff, were snuggled around her. Andi crept towards them, not wanting to frighten them by moving too quickly.

Natalie and Tristan followed. "They're so cute!" Andi whispered.

The Pet Finders knelt beside the basket while Mrs Talbot sat in an armchair. "How old are they?" Natalie asked.

"Two weeks, so their eyes are open now and they sometimes get out of the basket and have a sniff round," Shaun said. "But not for long. They like being with their mum."

Andi let Tooey sniff her hand, then gently touched the nearest pup; it was mostly black with a chocolate chest and tail. It rubbed its head against her hand and gave a shrill bark. It reminded Andi of the first time she'd seen Buddy. He'd been a little bit bigger than these pups, but he'd been just as cute and fluffy, and he'd had a way of looking up at Andi with his sweet brown eyes that made her pick him up and hug him every time.

Natalie turned to Shaun. "Is it OK to hold one?"

"Of course," Shaun replied. "It's good for them to be handled. It helps them get used to people."

"Come on, little one." Natalie slid her hand underneath one of the puppies and lifted her up. "You're a little beauty, aren't you? Oh!" She broke off in surprise. "Her tummy's cream. I've never seen a cream dachshund before."

"Well spotted," said Shaun. "It's a very rare colour, but the puppies' father, Snowy, is pure cream." He pointed to the sofa and Andi saw another dachshund curled up there. At first she thought he was asleep, but then she noticed that he had one eye slightly open.

He's watching out for the puppies, she thought, *to make sure we don't hurt them.*

"All but one of the puppies have some cream on them," Shaun said.

"How many boy and how many girl puppies are there?" Tristan asked, picking up a puppy with black-edged ears. He stroked its head and it licked his fingers with a tiny, pink tongue.

"Four girls and two boys," Shaun told him.

"Have you thought of names for them yet?" said Andi. She laughed as one of the puppies tumbled out of the basket, turned head-over-heels, and stood up, its eyes wide with surprise.

"Not yet. As we're breeding show dogs, naming them is pretty important. We usually raise about five or six pups a year and it's hard coming up with good show names for all of them." He grinned. "You'd be amazed at how long their names have to be, considering they're such tiny puppies! For example, Tooey's real name is Bluebell Lady Twoshoes, because she came from the Rose Kennels. All their puppy names begin with flowers."

"Have you got a theme for your dogs' names?" said Tristan.

Shaun nodded. "American States. All these pups' names will start with Vermont."

"How about Vermont Sugar for the puppy with the most cream fur?" Natalie suggested.

"And Vermont Kit-Kat for the chocolate-brown boy," Tristan added.

Shaun laughed. "Hmm, maybe not. We like to find names that sound fairly impressive. Snowy's really called Montana Snow Tiger! But we also like to be able to shorten them to something a bit more family-friendly."

Andi looked at Tristan and Natalie. "Do you remember the last time we tried to name a puppy?"

"Yes!" Natalie said. "That little golden Labrador we found in a ditch! She was so sweet."

"I haven't seen Mike for ages," mused Tristan. "I wonder how the puppy is."

The Pet Finders had saved the Labrador puppy's life when she'd been abandoned on the outskirts of Aldcliffe. She'd been adopted by a local postman, Mike Morgan.

"I wonder what Mike called her in the end," Tristan said.

"Not Fang, I bet," said Natalie.

Tristan shrugged. "OK, that wasn't one of my better ideas." He looked at the puppies. "Hey, I wonder if any of these have got sharp teeth."

"No, Tristan!" Natalie said sharply. "None of them

should be called Fang. Or Bruiser. Or any other name that sounds bad-tempered."

Shaun smiled. "I agree. We don't want to make our dogs sound hostile, even though dachshunds are famous for being brave in spite of their size. Do you know, I once heard of a miniature dachshund that took on a bull when its owner fell over in a field?"

"Did the dog win?" Tristan asked, impressed.

"It managed to draw the bull away and give its owner time to get up and out of the field. The dog escaped under the fence, so I suppose you could say it won."

"How about Vermont Brave Heart, then?" Tristan suggested. "Or Vermont Heroic Hunter?"

"Heroic Hunter," Shaun echoed. "That sounds quite good. And the puppy could be Hero for short. We'll have to see which one is bravest."

Andi leant over the basket to stroke the other puppies. There were two black-and-cream puppies playfully nipping each other's paws, and a chocolate-coloured puppy lying curled up beside his mother. His eyes were shut tight, as though he was determined to sleep through his sisters' game. Andi ran her finger down his velvety soft back. "Do you know, the way this one's lying all curled up reminds me of this image I saw everywhere in artwork when I was in Arizona. It was this hunchbacked flute-playing god called . . ."

Andi thought hard for a moment. "That's it! He was called Kokopelli!"

"Kokopelli," repeated Natalie. "That sounds cool."

Andi stroked the puppy's tiny ears. "Perhaps he could be called Vermont Kokopelli."

"And Koko for short," Tristan said. "That sounds nice and chocolatey to match his brown fur."

"Vermont Kokopelli," Shaun repeated. "Do you know, I think that name really suits him."

Andi felt a little thrill. She'd named a puppy! She grinned at her mum.

"Well done, Andi," Mrs Talbot said, smiling back.

The puppy woke up and lifted his head. "He knows we're talking about him," Natalie said.

The puppy sat up and put his front paws on Andi's hand. He didn't look anything like the hunchbacked flute-playing Tucson god now, but he was still adorable. She lifted him on to her lap. "Hello, Koko. What do you think of your new name?"

Koko licked Andi's finger with his pink tongue, then gave a high-pitched bark. Andi laughed. "I think he likes it."

The puppy closed his front paws round Andi's thumb as though they were tiny hands. He shook his head, making his silky ears flap, then rolled over with his tail wagging furiously.

Andi rubbed his tummy. "Look!" she said, peering more closely. "This little black patch on his tummy is shaped just like a keyhole!" She traced round it with her finger while Koko wriggled happily.

"Are you going to keep any of the puppies?" Natalie asked Shaun.

"No, they're all for sale. Eleanor's posted a photo of the litter on our website. We've had lots of congratulation messages from other breeders, thanks to the five puppies with cream in their coats. Everyone likes the rare colours! But we're in no hurry to sell them, so we've got plenty of time to find the best homes."

"How do you decide who'd make a good owner?" Tristan wanted to know.

"Well, it's best if they've owned dogs before, especially dachshunds. We never let our dogs go to anyone who doesn't know something about the breed. And they need to understand how much commitment it takes to be a dog owner."

"It sounds like applying for a job," Tristan joked.

"It is," Shaun agreed. "A full-time, twenty-four hours a day job."

The door opened and a slim woman with a heart-shaped face and a dimpling smile came in carrying two bulging bags of groceries. "Phew!" she exclaimed, setting them down. "Carrying shopping is better than a work-out at the gym!"

"This is my wife, Eleanor," said Shaun. "Eleanor, this is Judy Talbot." He gestured towards Andi's mum, who stood up and shook hands with Eleanor. "And this is Andi, Tristan and Natalie."

"Hello," said Eleanor, smiling. "What do you think of the puppies?"

"They're gorgeous," Andi said. She rubbed Koko's tummy again and he wrinkled his nose at her.

"We've named this little chap," Shaun said, pointing to Koko. "Vermont Kokopelli. Or Koko, if you prefer."

Eleanor's green eyes shone. "What a beautiful name!"

"Andi thought of it," Shaun told her. He glanced at his watch. "I'd better get going. I'm playing squash in twenty minutes." He shot out of the room.

"Are you all OK here while I go and get changed?" Eleanor asked.

"You bet!" Tristan said.

"Great! We don't like to leave the puppies on their own, but I'm sure they'll be fine with you."

When Eleanor had gone out, Tristan picked up one of the puppies – a girl with more cream on her than the others – and let her snuggle against his chest. "It's amazing that Shaun and Eleanor never leave the puppies alone." He grinned. "It sounds as though the Pet Finders are never going to be needed here!"

Chapter Four

Andi thought about Tooey's puppies as she walked to school next morning, picturing the way Koko kept rolling over to have his tummy stroked. She'd have to email Nina and tell her she'd named a purebred show puppy!

While they were waiting for Mr Dixon to call the register that morning, Andi joined her friends at Cinnamon's cage.

"I've brought him some chunks of carrot," Howard said, opening his rucksack and pulling out some books about hamsters and a very crumpled homework sheet.

"Are you still doing hamster research, Howard?" Andi asked, leafing through one of the books.

Howard nodded. "Did you know hamsters need a block of wood to gnaw, to stop their teeth growing too much? I'm going to buy Cinnamon one on Saturday."

With a flourish he produced a plastic bag of carrot from the bottom of his rucksack, like a magician whisking a rabbit out of a top hat. "Here it is." He put it into the drawer that held Cinnamon's food.

"Who's going to feed him today?" Natalie said.

"We should draw up a rota," Howard suggested, "so everyone can have a turn. Otherwise we'll just argue about it." He looked darkly at Kelly. "Some people have already had two turns while the rest of us haven't even had one."

"You can count me out," said Larissa. "I'm not going anywhere near that hamster." She still had a plaster on her finger where Cinnamon had bitten her.

"Cinnamon won't bite you again," Andi said. "It was only because your hands smelt of apple."

"You can help me," said Howard. He grinned. "I'll do all the dangerous stuff and you can refill the water bottle."

"OK. But I am *not* putting my fingers inside the cage again."

Mr Dixon told everyone to sit down. "A rota is a good idea," he agreed. "Everyone write your name on a piece of paper while I call the register. Afterwards, we'll draw names to see who'll be looking after Cinnamon today."

He collected the pieces of paper and put them in a

42

tin, then pulled one out. "Today Tanya will be in charge of Cinnamon," he announced.

Andi was disappointed that she hadn't been picked. She waited hopefully as Mr Dixon drew out the name for the next day. "I hope it's me," Howard whispered.

"Robert," Mr Dixon said, reading the next slip of paper. He went on drawing names until everyone in the class had been allocated a day to look after Cinnamon. Andi was in charge next Friday, the day after Larissa.

"I'm not sure I want to do this!" Larissa groaned.

"Don't worry," Howard said. "I'll give you a hand." He beamed. "That way I get two turns. And Cinnamon will have two days of being held by someone who knows not to squeeze him."

"Thanks, Howard." Larissa turned to Andi. "How's your Buddy project going?"

"It's not exactly about Buddy, any more."

"Oh? What are you doing it on, then?"

"It's a secret." Since she'd started Musical Freestyling classes, Andi had changed her mind about the subject of her project. She'd decided to call it "Talented Pets" now. Buddy would still be the star, of course, but Andi planned to include photos of Whisper, too. The highlight of the project would be a video of her and Bud doing their Musical Freestyling, and she was spending every spare minute practising. Remembering what Mr Dixon had said about including maths in her project, she was planning to work out how much it would cost if she took Buddy to Freestyling classes for six months, nine months, and a whole year. And for English, she was writing a poem called *Dancing Dogs*.

"You can tell *us* what it's about," Howard said. "We won't say a word."

Andi shook her head. "Nope. You'll have to wait and see."

The bell rang. "Time for PE," Mr Dixon said.

Andi snatched up her rucksack and darted to the door: PE was her favourite lesson. As she ran into the corridor, she collided with Tanya McLennan.

"Look where you're going!" Tanya snapped as her rucksack skidded along the corridor.

"Sorry," Andi panted. She began to pick up Tanya's books and pens.

"Wait – I'm sorry I snapped," Tanya said.

She looked pale and strained, Andi thought, surprised: Tanya was normally one of the most cheery people in the class. "Are you OK?"

Tanya shrugged. "I suppose so."

Andi could see there was something wrong. "Can I do anything to help?"

"Not unless you can provide a teddy bear-finding service!"

Andi finished picking up Tanya's things and put them into her rucksack. "Is there a problem with the bear you were going to buy for Marie's birthday?"

Tanya nodded miserably. "The toy shop's sold out. I don't suppose you've got any bright ideas about what I can get instead?"

They reached the changing room. "I'm not sure," Andi said, hanging her rucksack on an empty peg. "Marie likes animals, doesn't she?"

"Yes, that's why the bear would have been so perfect."

"What about a toy farm?"

Tanya shook her head. "She's already got one. And Mum gets cross about her leaving the little plastic animals all over the place, so I can't buy her any more." She shrugged. "Don't worry, I'll think of something. But let me know if you come up with any ideas, won't you?"

For the next few days, Andi practised Musical Freestyling with Buddy whenever she could. She also worked hard on her poem. She was already halfway through and she planned to type it into the computer, print it out, and decorate it with drawings of Buddy, Whisper and Jet dancing.

On Saturday afternoon, Andi, Tristan and Natalie

met near their school to take Buddy and Jet for a walk in the park. It was a bright day but the wind was cold, and Andi tied her scarf more tightly as they set off along the road. "Do you mind if we go a different way?" Tristan asked. "My mum and dad are selling some new flats in Stanbury Road and I'd like to have a look at them. They sound really cool!" Tristan's parents ran an estate agency.

"OK," Andi agreed.

"As long as it's not miles out of our way," Natalie warned. "I'm not trekking five hundred miles just to look at a block of flats."

"No, it's hardly any further," Tristan said.

Tristan told them about some new baby hamsters that had just arrived at Paws for Thought as they walked. "They're so cute," he said. "Really tiny and fluffy."

Suddenly they heard paws racing towards them and a gorgeous golden face leapt up at Andi.

"Hey, girl!" Andi exclaimed. It was the rescued Labrador that Mike the postman had adopted. Andi crouched down and the young dog jumped up and planted her feet on Andi's knees. "You remember me, don't you? What a clever girl!" Andi praised her.

The Labrador barked, then jumped up at Natalie and Tristan, her feathery tail wagging furiously.

"It's really good to see you again!" said Tristan, ruffling her ears. "You look great!"

Buddy and Jet leapt around the young dog, barking with excitement.

Mike jogged round the corner. "Hey, I haven't seen you for ages. How are you all?" His postbag was bouncing on his hip and he was carrying a large rectangular parcel under his arm.

"We're fine, Mike," Tristan replied. "Where have you been?"

"I took a few weeks off for some training in Scotland. It was amazing! All that running up and down mountains. And Laura loved it, too."

"Laura? Is that her name?" Andi was delighted to hear the beautiful dog had a name at last. It really suited her, too!

At the mention of her name, Laura tried to climb right on to Andi's lap, but she was so excited that she scrabbled too far and fell off the other side, landing on Natalie's feet.

"Mind you don't scratch Nat's shoes," Tristan warned. "Or you'll be in big trouble."

"Oh, she's cute enough to get away with anything," said Natalie. She ran her fingers through the puppy's soft yellow coat. "She looks really fit, Mike."

"Thanks," said Mike. "She's good company, too. I

can't imagine what it would be like not having her around all the time. There's just one problem with taking her marathon-training: she's better at it than I am!"

Andi laughed. "She's got four legs. You've only got two." She straightened up. "That's a big parcel, Mike. Do you want a hand with it?"

"Don't worry, it's not heavy. According to the label, it's a hamster cage. Empty, I hope!" He grinned and checked the address. "Actually, it's for this house here."

Andi noticed the name on the parcel. "It's for Tanya McLennan. She's in my class. Shall we deliver it for you?"

"Thanks, that would be a big help. I've promised Laura a ten-kilometre run as soon as I've finished, and I can tell she's itching to get going!"

He handed the box to Andi. As he had said, it wasn't heavy, just bulky, with rather sharp edges that dug into Andi's hip. She was glad she only had to carry it as far as Tanya's front door. They said goodbye to Mike and Laura, making a special fuss of the gorgeous little dog, and headed up the path. The house was modern and it looked roomy, with tall front windows.

Natalie rang the bell. "I hope Tanya invites us in to look at her hamster," she said.

Tanya opened the door. "Er, hi," she said, obviously surprised to see them.

"We're delivering this parcel for the postman," Andi told her, handing it over. "It's a hamster cage. I didn't know you had a hamster, Tanya."

"I haven't," Tanya said quickly. "The cage is for a mouse."

"A mouse! Can we see it?" Tristan asked.

"No, sorry. I haven't got it yet. Thanks for delivering the cage." Tanya put the box on the floor and started to shut the door. "Sorry I can't invite you in but I'm a bit busy just now. Bye."

Andi frowned as the door closed. "She really *is* in a hurry!"

Natalie shrugged. "Well, at least we helped Mike out. And it was lovely to see Laura again!"

They set off along the pavement again.

"I wonder why Tanya didn't buy the cage at Paws for Thought," Tristan mused. "She must have paid loads of postage buying it by mail order."

"Never mind about that," Natalie said. "How much further is it to these flats, Tris? They are in Aldcliffe, aren't they? If we keep going much longer, we'll end up in Wales!"

Chapter Five

To Andi's disappointment, Shaun and Whisper missed the next Freestyling class. Andi was sure Buddy was disappointed too – he kept looking round for his dance partner as they practised their moves. When Andi asked Chloe if Shaun was OK, the instructor explained that he'd had to stay at home because someone had arranged to see Tooey's puppies. Andi felt a pang of excitement that one of the gorgeous little dogs might be about to find a brilliant home. She hoped Koko would put on a good show for the prospective buyer!

Heading home after the Freestyling class, Andi saw a sign in the window of the bookshop on Main Street. "Oh!" she said, stopping so abruptly that Buddy jerked on the end of his head. "Dale Savage is doing an author visit!"

Dale Savage was the presenter of her favourite TV

show, *The Wolf at Home*. It explained the natural behaviour of dogs, showing how all their habits were based on survival instincts from their wild past. Andi had been fascinated to learn that Buddy chased after balls and sticks because he had a deeply-rooted instinct that his wolf ancestors had needed to catch food by running after it.

"I can't wait to read his new book, *Pet Wolf*!" said Natalie. "His show is fantastic! Do you know why Jet turns round in his basket before he goes to sleep? It's because dogs in ancient times used to circle to flatten the grass they wanted to sleep on."

"Buddy does that, too," Andi said, thinking about the way he turned on the spot before settling in the crook of her legs every night when she went to bed.

"Jet used to do it on my lap when he was a puppy," Natalie said. "I wouldn't want him sitting on me now. I'd be squashed flat!" She patted him. "But you can sit *beside* me any time, boy."

They walked past the road where the Carters lived, and Andi hesitated. "Do you think we could call in and see if any of the puppies have found a new home?"

"Good idea," said Natalie. She glanced at Andi. "You'll miss Koko if he's sold, won't you?"

"I suppose I will," Andi admitted. "But he deserves to have a really special owner all to himself."

Shaun Carter opened the door. "Oh, hi. I thought you might be the chap who's coming to look at the puppies. He's running late, but that's not a problem because it means Eleanor's home in time to meet him." He frowned. "We weren't expecting to see you today, were we?"

"Er, no," said Andi. "But Chloe told us that someone was coming to see the puppies and I wanted to know how things went."

Shaun grinned. "Checking to make sure Koko gets a good owner, eh? Come on through. Buddy and Jet will have to wait in the kitchen, I'm afraid, because the puppies haven't had their vaccinations yet."

Jet flopped down beside the cooker and Buddy went to lap from Whisper's water bowl. "We won't be long," Andi promised as she shut the door.

Eleanor was in the living room, kneeling on the floor beside the dog basket. "Hello there," she said, shifting so they could join her.

"Hello," said Andi. "Thanks for letting us see the puppies again." She crouched down and laughed as Koko gently nibbled her finger, then shook his head, making his ears flap.

Eleanor smiled. "It's easy to see which one's your favourite!"

"And I love this little one best," said Natalie. She

lifted up the chocolate-and-cream girl. "Have you chosen a name for her yet?"

Eleanor nodded. "Vermont Maple Leaf. Leaf for short."

"Leaf," Natalie echoed. "It's perfect!"

Eleanor glanced at the clock. "I hope this man's coming. He sounds ideal." She fetched a sheet of paper from the table. "Would you like to see the photos of the dachshunds he used to own?"

Andi admired the two images on the printout. One was a sleek black-and-tan, long-haired dachshund gazing straight at the camera, while the other picture showed a smooth-coated fawn dachshund with a paler neck and tummy. Both looked fit and healthy.

The doorbell rang. Shaun went to answer it and came back with a friendly-looking man in his early twenties. He had red hair, warm blue eyes and a broad smile. "Hello. You must be Mrs Carter." He shook hands with Eleanor. "I'm Zan Kirby. Thanks for letting me see the puppies. Will it be possible to meet their mum and dad, too, and have a look at your whole set-up? The best way to tell how a pup will turn out is to see how its parents are cared for, I always say."

"Absolutely!" Shaun Carter agreed. "It makes my blood boil the way some people buy dogs from puppy farms without a thought for the animals' welfare."

Andi and Natalie put the puppies gently back into the basket and stood up to make room for Zan Kirby. "Thanks," he said. "Are you two choosing a puppy? You look a bit young. Shouldn't your mum and dad be here with you?"

"We're just friends," Natalie explained.

"Oh, I see." Zan let Tooey sniff his hand before he tried to touch any of the pups.

Well, he certainly knows about dogs, Andi thought approvingly.

"He's a cute little chap," Zan commented, picking up Koko. The puppy snuggled against his chest, wagging his tail. Then he reached out and held Zan's thumb with his front paws, just as he'd done with Andi's.

Zan laughed. "I've never known a dog do that before."

Andi was thrilled Zan had picked out her favourite. She watched Zan gently check him over, looking at his eyes and teeth.

"He seems healthy. And his teeth are sharp enough!" Zan added as Koko gave him a playful nip.

"You know the puppies won't be ready to leave us until they're eight weeks old and have had their first jabs?" Eleanor Carter checked. "I've already booked their appointment with Mr Harvey, our vet. You can check the exact date on our website if you like."

Zan nodded. "But I'll need to pay you a deposit to reserve the puppy I'm interested in. Right?"

"Yes."

Zan set Koko down on the floor and watched as the puppy tried to clamber on to his lap. "He's a determined little one. That's good. It's a nice quality in a dog." He picked Koko up again. "I'd like a little more time before I make up my mind. Would it be OK to come again to make sure this little chap and I are right for each other?"

"Of course," said Shaun. He glanced at Eleanor, and Andi could tell they were impressed.

Zan put Koko back in the basket. "I'll see you soon," he said, standing up. He shook hands with Shaun and Eleanor, smiled at Andi and Natalie, and headed for the door.

"We should go too," said Natalie. "Thanks for letting us see the puppies again."

"You can come whenever you like. It's good for the pups to meet lots of new people." Eleanor reached down to pet Leaf's head. "Zan looks like he'd be a fantastic owner, but it's such a shame we can't keep them all!"

On Thursday, it was Larissa's turn to look after Cinnamon. As soon as they went into the classroom at the start of the day, Howard fetched the cage and set it down on Andi's table. "You change the water, Larissa, and I'll do everything else."

"I won't have to put my hand in the cage?" Larissa said, eyeing it anxiously.

"Nope. Super-Howard will risk life and limb by changing Cinnamon's bedding and topping up his food bowl!" Howard zoomed across the room to fetch the new bedding, with one arm stretched out in front of him like Superman. Andi laughed. Howard was such a comedian!

The shredded paper rustled and Cinnamon peeped out of his little house. "Who wants to hold him while I change his bedding?" said Howard, returning with a huge bag of bedding. "Only people who know how to hold hamsters properly need apply."

"I'll do it!" Andi offered. She held out her hands as Howard dumped the bag of bedding on the table and tried to open the cage door.

"Ouch!" he said, pulling his hand away.

"Has Cinnamon bitten you?" Larissa gasped.

"No. I caught my finger in the door. It's very stiff."

"We ought to get it fixed," said Tanya McLennan, coming over to see what was going on. "It would be awful if Cinnamon got stuck in there one day."

"Perhaps the caretaker could do it," Andi suggested.

"Good idea," Tanya agreed.

"Yeah. I'll ask him at lunchtime." Howard yanked the door open and reached into the cage. Cinnamon climbed happily on to Howard's hand so he could be lifted out. Kelly had been in charge of taming him. To start with, she'd put a cup into the cage and let Cinnamon climb inside. Then she'd lifted him and the cup out and given him a slice of carrot to tempt him on to her hand. Now, he was tame enough not to need the cup any more: he climbed straight on to a hand when it appeared inside his cage.

Howard held his hand next to Andi's and Cinnamon stepped across. He sat up on his hind legs and washed his whiskers, gazing at Andi with his beady black eyes.

Andi stroked his tan-and-white fur with one finger. He felt soft and warm. "He's so cute!" she murmured. "Don't you even want to stroke him, Larissa?"

Larissa made a face. "No thanks! Hamsters are definitely *not* my favourite animals. But that doesn't mean I'll let him get thirsty." She unclipped Cinnamon's water bottle and went to the sink to refill it.

"He's really tame now," Tanya said. "He'll go to anyone." She held out a sunflower seed and the hamster took it in his tiny paws, then tucked it into his pouch.

When the cage had been cleaned out, Andi put Cinnamon back inside. He crawled straight inside his

house, rearranging the bedding with his teeth as he went.

"Time for history," Mr Dixon announced.

Larissa closed the cage and Howard carried it back to the corner. "There you are, Cinnamon." He glanced at the clock. "Hey, can someone remind me that I've got a dentist's appointment today? My mum's picking me up at half past ten, and I forgot about the last one."

Andi rolled her eyes. "Trust you, Howard!"

"I'm just glad you didn't have to go before we'd finished cleaning out Cinnamon," Larissa said with feeling. "I definitely wouldn't have liked doing it by myself."

At the end of the day, Andi went back to her classroom to get her maths book. Larissa was with her, talking about how difficult it was to sculpt her aunt's cat in clay for the art part of her pet project.

In the classroom, Chen and Kelly were leaning over Cinnamon's cage.

"Is Cinnamon awake?" Andi asked.

"There's no sign of him. He must be curled up in bed," said Kelly.

"He's probably pining for Howard," Chen joked. He peered closer and frowned. "Normally his bedding moves a tiny bit when he's asleep, but it's completely still."

Andi hurried over, suddenly feeling anxious. She opened the cage and tapped the side of the house. "Cinnamon! Cinnamon?" She was reluctant to wake him up if he was having a nap, but she wanted to be sure he was fine before she went home.

There was still no movement.

Andi shifted the paper so she could see right inside the house. "He's not there!" she gasped.

Larissa's face turned as white as a sheet of paper and she sat down heavily on a chair.

"What's up?" asked Natalie, coming into the classroom.

"Cinnamon's gone!" Andi exclaimed. She raised her voice to make herself heard as more people came in to collect their rucksacks before going home. "Listen, everyone. Cinnamon's missing. We'll all have to search the classroom."

"Slowly and carefully," Natalie added. "We don't want to scare him."

"We need to look in our bags," Andi went on. "Hamsters are pretty good at climbing. So even if your bag hasn't been on the floor, he might have found a way into it."

61

"And we need to look in cupboards and underneath everything," Natalie put in.

Everyone began to search, tipping out school bags, peering under radiators and delving into cupboards. "We don't know much about finding tiny indoor pets," Andi whispered to Natalie as they lay down flat to peer under the bookcase. All their classmates knew that she, Natalie and Tristan were the Pet Finders, and they'd be relying on them to find the little hamster. Andi hated the thought of letting them down.

"I think I can see him!" Chen shouted from the back of the room. "He's under this cupboard."

Andi and Natalie hurried over, but before they reached him Chen groaned. "False alarm. It's a ball of orange wool." He held it up. "It must have been there since we did macramé last term."

With everyone helping, it didn't take long to search the room. Cinnamon was nowhere to be seen.

"What do we do now?" Chen asked. Everyone turned to Andi and Natalie expectantly.

"I'm not sure," Andi admitted. "We've never had to find a missing hamster before."

"I think I've read something about lost hamsters on a website," Kelly said. She ran to the computer desk and logged on. "Let me check the sites I bookmarked."

Andi and Natalie looked over her shoulder as she called up a hamster website. It said that escaped hamsters usually found a place to hide until night time. "Lost hamsters often come out and wander around when it gets dark," Andi read.

"That's no help," said Chen. "We won't be here to catch Cinnamon then."

With a start, Andi saw that Larissa was still sitting at their table with her hands over her face. Her shoulders were shaking and Andi realized she was crying. She went over and put her arm round Larissa. "Don't worry. We'll find him. He can't have gone far."

Larissa just shook her head and carried on crying. Andi couldn't help feeling a bit surprised by Larissa's reaction – after all, she was hardly Cinnamon's biggest fan.

Natalie was reading a website over Kelly's shoulder. "Look, we can make a trap," she said. "A gentle one," she added when someone gasped. "The website shows you what to do."

Mr Dixon came in. "What's going on? Do you all love school so much that you can't bear to go home?"

"Cinnamon's disappeared," Natalie told him.

His smile faded. "Oh no. We'll have to organize a search."

"We've already done that," said Andi. "But Kelly's

found a website with some tips on how to catch escaped hamsters." She squeezed Larissa's arm, then stood up so she could see the computer screen too.

"First we need a bucket," said Kelly, running her finger down the list of tips on the screen.

Mr Dixon sent Chen to ask the caretaker for one.

"We'll need wood chippings from Cinnamon's cage," Natalie continued. "And some food."

"And books," Kelly added.

"Books?" echoed Robert. "For Cinnamon to read?"

Nobody laughed. Looking round, Andi saw she was surrounded by worried faces.

"It's to build a staircase up to the top of the bucket," Kelly explained.

By the time Chen came back with the bucket, the books had been piled up. "Put the bucket beside the books, please," said Kelly.

Chen did as she said, though from his puzzled expression it was clear he didn't know what was going on.

"Now, Nat, you need to tip the wood chippings into the bucket and scatter some food on top," Kelly went on. "Hopefully Cinnamon will smell the food and wood chippings," she explained. "It should remind him of home, so he'll climb up the books and drop into the bucket."

"Excellent!" Chen whooped. "He'll never get out of there! That's a great website you've found, Kelly."

"Now the trap's set up, would someone like to tell me what happened?" said Mr Dixon.

"Cinnamon must have escaped while we were out of the room," Andi told him. "His cage was empty when we came back from our last class." She showed Mr Dixon the cage door. "It's really stiff, but I'm sure nobody would have left it undone . . ." She tailed off, remembering Larissa's reaction to Cinnamon's disappearance. Andi looked round for her, wondering if she could have left the cage open by mistake, but Larissa wasn't there. "That's weird," she remarked to Natalie. "Larissa's gone already."

"Has she?" Natalie raised her eyebrows. "Considering Cinnamon was her responsibility today, you'd think she could have stayed to help with the trap."

"Perhaps she had an appointment after school," Andi said. She really hoped Larissa hadn't left the cage door open, but it would explain why she seemed so upset. From the look on Natalie's face, she was obviously thinking the same thing.

The class repacked their bags and cleared up quickly. "I hope we catch Cinnamon," Andi said, as she and Natalie walked out of school. She shivered, remembering the time she'd lost Buddy when she'd first moved to Aldcliffe. She'd been worried sick. And poor Cinnamon was so much tinier and more helpless than Buddy. "Let's hope the bucket trap works," she said, crossing her fingers for luck.

"I'll phone Tristan when I get home and tell him what's going on," Natalie said. "He's a Pet Finder, so he should be involved in finding Cinnamon."

They reached the end of her road. "See you tomorrow," Andi called, hitching her rucksack on to her shoulder. Wherever Cinnamon was, she hoped the cute little hamster had found a safe, snug corner for the night.

Chapter Six

"You're very quiet, Andi," Mrs Talbot said, while Andi was feeding Buddy that evening. "What's up?"

"I keep thinking about Cinnamon."

Her mum patted her arm. "He'll be OK, I'm sure. It's pretty common for hamsters to escape and they usually turn up the next day. I bet he'll be in that catching bucket when you get to school tomorrow."

Andi forced a smile.

"Are you going to practise your Freestyle later?" said Mrs Talbot.

Andi shook her head. "I don't feel like practising tonight. Is it OK if I email Dad to tell him about Cinnamon?" Andi's Dad was really interested in the Pet Finders Club since he'd helped look for Nina's kittens in Tucson.

"Of course, darling."

Andi ran upstairs with Buddy at her heels. He lay

across her feet as soon as she sat down at the computer. He seemed subdued, as though he could sense Andi's anxiety. And she *was* worried. It was strange to be working on the case of a missing pet that she knew so well. She typed quickly, telling her dad about Cinnamon's disappearance. Then she described the new dachshund friends she'd made. She decided to attach a picture so he'd know how cute they were.

As she didn't have a picture of Tooey's puppies, Andi decided to look up some sites on miniature dachshunds. She found a picture of some dachshund puppies and attached it to her email – even though they weren't as gorgeous as Tooey's babies. She was about to close the website when a picture of a black-and-tan dachshund with a long silky coat caught her eye.

"This dog looks familiar!" she said out loud.

At the sound of her voice, Buddy jumped up and planted his paws on her knee. Andi rubbed his ears while she peered at the photo more closely. "Maybe it's related to Tooey or Snowy," she guessed. "I'll ask the Carters. I bet they recognize all their puppies, even when they're grown up." She printed the photo to show them later.

As she lay in bed, trying to go to sleep, Andi took her mind off Cinnamon by thinking about Koko instead. She hoped she'd be able to visit him again soon. She pictured the way the little pup had rolled over on her lap so she could rub his tummy. That patch of keyhole-shaped black fur was so unusual, and she loved the way he held her thumb with his tiny paws. He was adorable!

"But not as adorable as you, Bud," Andi said loyally, reaching down to the end of the bed to stroke his silky ears.

Next morning, Tristan, Andi and Natalie met up on the steps before the start of school.

"Cold or what?" Tristan gasped, turning up the collar of his jacket. "I hope Cinnamon managed to keep warm last night. I spoke to Christine after you rang me, Nat, and she said he should be fine as long as he doesn't get too cold."

"A catching bucket with plenty of wood chippings in it should be warm enough for him," Natalie said, crossing her fingers for luck.

The bell rang and they made a dash for the door. "I hope Miss Ashworthy doesn't catch you, Tris," Andi said as they hurried along the corridor. Tristan's strict teacher wouldn't be pleased to find him going the wrong way at the start of the school day.

Tristan shrugged. "What's a couple of breaktime

detentions to a famous Pet Finder?" All the same, he glanced over his shoulder to check that Miss Ashworthy wasn't behind them.

They reached the classroom. The catching bucket was standing in the middle of the room, just as they'd left it.

Andi reached the bucket and peered in . . .

It was EMPTY!

"Cinnamon's not in the bucket," Andi said heavily.

She heard a startled cry and turned round to see Larissa spin round in the doorway and run down the corridor.

Andi darted after her, but there were so many people streaming towards their classrooms that she was already out of sight. Andi went back into class, determined to ask Larissa some questions next time she saw her. A few people were peering under the cupboards around the wall. Others were sitting at their desks, talking in subdued voices.

"I'd better go," Tristan said. "Let's meet up later to work out a plan for finding Cinnamon." He ran out of the room, nearly colliding with Mr Dixon.

"Careful, Tristan," he warned.

"Sorry, sir!" Tristan hurtled away down the corridor.

"Where's Howard?" Kelly asked as she sat down beside Andi.

"He's going to be gutted when he hears Cinnamon's missing," said Chen.

"I know," Andi agreed. "I'll give him a ring." She took out her mobile and looked up his number. "Howard, is that you?" she said, when a rather muffled voice answered.

"Yes."

"This is Andi. Are you OK?"

"No. My teeth hurt."

"Listen, Howard, I've got some bad news. Cinnamon's disappeared. He got out of his cage yesterday."

"No!"

"Andi, put your phone away," Mr Dixon called. "I'm about to take the register."

"Sorry, Howard, I've got to go. See you." Andi rang off.

Larissa came in. Her eyes were red-rimmed from crying and she deliberately didn't look at the empty hamster cage as she hurried across the classroom and sat down.

"Are you OK?" Andi whispered. The rest of her questions would have to wait until later.

Larissa fished a tissue out of her pocket and blew her nose. "I . . . I suppose so."

The class sat quietly while the register was called. Looking round the room, Andi saw the same worried expressions on every face. Where had Cinnamon got to? And how were they ever going to find him? He was the smallest pet they'd ever had to search for, and if he wasn't in the classroom, he could be anywhere in the school – or beyond.

At morning break, Andi looked round for Larissa. She was peeling a banana at the edge of the playground, where it joined the playing field. As Andi headed towards her, Natalie ran up and whispered fiercely in her ear. "I'm sure Larissa knows something about Cinnamon's disappearance. In detective shows, the person who finds the body is usually the prime suspect, and Larissa was there when you noticed Cinnamon had gone!"

"Oh, don't be silly! There hasn't been a crime!" Andi said. Natalie and Larissa weren't great friends, but it sounded as if Nat was accusing Larissa of letting Cinnamon out on purpose.

Tristan was playing football in the middle of the playground. He stopped when he heard Andi say "crime" and jogged over. "What's up?"

Natalie told him she was suspicious of the way Larissa had been behaving since Cinnamon had disappeared. Tristan nodded thoughtfully. "She might have stolen him," he suggested.

"Larissa doesn't even like hamsters!" Andi said. She wanted to ask Larissa why she was so upset about Cinnamon, but she didn't think her friend was a thief!

"So she says," Natalie said. "But that could be her cover story. Maybe she loves them but she pretended to be scared of Cinnamon so no one would suspect her when she stole him."

"Larissa would not steal the class hamster!"

"Then why does she keep crying?" Natalie pointed out. "It looks like a guilty conscience to me."

"Perhaps she realizes she shouldn't have done it, but it's too late to do anything about it," Tristan suggested.

Andi couldn't deny it was odd the way Larissa had reacted. "I think she could know more than she's letting on," she admitted. "That's why I'm going to talk to her."

"I'm coming with you," Tristan said.

"And me!" Natalie said.

Andi raised her eyebrows. "Do you think that's a good idea, Nat?"

"This is a missing-pet investigation," Natalie reminded her. "In case you'd forgotten, I'm a member of the Pet Finders Club too."

Andi knew there was no point arguing. "OK, but don't start shining a torch in Larissa's eyes or anything."

They ran over to Larissa just as she finished the last mouthful of her banana.

"We want to talk to you about Cinnamon," Tristan began.

"When exactly did you last see him?" Natalie demanded.

Larissa shrugged helplessly. "I . . . Um . . ."

"You were supposed to be looking after him on the day he vanished," Natalie reminded her.

Andi gave Natalie a hard stare: going on at Larissa as though she was a wanted criminal wouldn't help them find out what had happened to Cinnamon! "You must feel really bad about Cinnamon disappearing when you were in charge, Larissa," she said sympathetically. "But you're acting as though the whole thing was your fault."

To her dismay, Larissa started crying again. "I'm so sorry! I didn't mean for Cinnamon to run away," she sobbed. "But it *was* my fault. And now we'll never find him again!"

Andi put her arm round Larissa. "Did you forget to close the cage door at lunchtime?"

Larissa cried harder than ever.

"You can tell me," Andi said. She took a packet of tissues out of her rucksack and gave one to Larissa. "Here."

Larissa blew her nose. "I d . . . didn't f . . . feed Cinnamon at l . . . lunchtime. I was s . . . scared of being b . . . bitten and I couldn't find Howard anywhere. I j . . . just went to lunch with everyone else. Cinnamon must have escaped because he was hungry." She covered her face with her hands.

Andi started to laugh, then quickly turned the laugh into a cough as Larissa looked up at her in dismay. Andi knew there wasn't anything to laugh at: Cinnamon was still missing, after all. But Larissa really didn't need to blame herself. "Hamsters don't eat separate meals," Andi explained. "He wouldn't have got out because he'd finished his breakfast and wanted some lunch."

"They nibble little mouthfuls from their pot of food all through the day," Tristan put in.

"It's what hamsters do in the wild," Natalie said. To Andi's relief, she sounded much more gentle now. "They forage for food when they're hungry. Cinnamon always has food in his bowl. He couldn't have been hungry, even if it wasn't as full as usual."

"And he usually stores some food in his cheek pouches, too," Andi said. "That's why he has such a fat face."

Larissa looked up. Her face was wet with tears. "So it might not have been my fault that he got out?"

"Definitely not," Andi said firmly. "Cinnamon probably didn't even notice his bowl hadn't been topped up." She gave Larissa another tissue.

"Thanks." Larissa wiped her eyes. "You've made me feel loads better. But we still need to find Cinnamon, don't we?"

"Yes," Andi agreed. "We still need to find Cinnamon." And if he'd got out of the school, the catching bucket wasn't going to help at all.

Straight after school, Andi and Natalie hurried to the Carters' house. Shaun had phoned Andi to ask if they would keep an eye on the puppies while he and Eleanor got ready for a dinner party that evening. Andi was happy to help, especially because the puppies had been due to have their first vaccinations today and she wanted to check that Koko was OK. Tristan couldn't come because he was helping out at Paws for Thought.

Eleanor Carter looked rather flustered when she opened the door to Andi and Natalie. She had one arm hooked in the sleeve of a blue jacket. "Hello, girls, have you come to see the puppies?"

"Yes. Shaun phoned to ask if we could watch them for you, because you're really busy." Andi said.

"Oh, wonderful. Thank you for coming! Come in."

Inside, the house smelt deliciously of chocolate. "It's a Black Forest gateau," Eleanor explained when she noticed Andi sniffing. "We've got guests coming for dinner. It's bad timing really, because I got delayed at the vet's. It looked as though every puppy in Aldcliffe was there today. And Shaun's had to work late, so I ended up rushing home to let Zan Kirby see the pups again."

"Has he made up his mind about Koko?" Andi asked.

"Not yet, but he's obviously really interested. To be honest, I could have done without him coming today, with dinner to prepare, but he looks like such a good owner that I didn't want to put him off."

Tooey sat up when she saw Andi and Natalie come into the living room.

Andi knelt down and stroked her. "Hello, girl."

Koko was lying a little apart from his brother and sisters. He was asleep but he opened his eyes and tried to sit up when Andi stroked his velvety fur with one finger. She scooped him up and laid him on her lap. "I wonder if I can get him to do that nose-wrinkling thing again," she said, rubbing his velvety tummy. She watched him closely, but he lay still, looking up at her with half-closed eyes.

"Are you still feeling a bit sleepy, boy?" Andi murmured.

Natalie picked up Leaf. "You can see why people like cream dachshunds. Leaf's patches are a sort of buttery colour and they really stand out." The puppy nibbled her finger. "She's so cute," Natalie giggled, "but I don't think Jet would be too pleased if he had to share me."

Andi turned Koko over and held out her thumb, hoping he'd grab on to it with his paws again. He sniffed her thumb, then snuggled down. "Is he all right, do you think?" she said. "He's really dopey today."

Natalie shrugged. "It's probably the effects of his jab. Jet was like that when he had his first vaccinations. He was OK the next day, though."

"Perhaps going out of the house to the vet's was a shock," Andi mused, tracing the outline of the black patches on Koko's back. "He didn't know the rest of the world existed until today!" She smoothed the fur on the top of his head, then put him back into the basket beside Tooey. "I'll let you sleep, Koko. I expect you're too tired to play today."

Tooey stood up, whining. She climbed out of the basket and trotted over to Andi.

"What's up, girl?" said Andi.

"Maybe she's getting tired of having the puppies

round her all the time," Natalie suggested. "It must be a pain, never having a moment to yourself."

"Don't worry, girl," Andi said, stroking Tooey's nose. "They'll all be sold in a few weeks and then you can have as much time to yourself as you want."

"Should we practise our Freestyling tonight?" said Natalie. "We could fetch Buddy and you could come back to my house."

"Good idea. Let's go now, or we won't have time to go through all our moves." Andi bent over the basket again. "Bye, Koko. I'll see you again soon." She ruffled his ears but he gave a tiny wail of complaint. "Sorry, boy." Andi left him to snooze and stood up.

Natalie laid Leaf back in the basket. As she and Andi headed for the door, Tooey trotted after them.

"You stay in here, girl," Andi said, pushing her gently back inside. She closed the door behind her. "We're just going now, if that's OK," she said to Eleanor, popping her head into the kitchen.

Eleanor Carter smiled. "That half hour away from the puppies has been a real help. I've almost finished in here." She brushed flour from her hands and followed them to the front door. "Thanks for coming. See you again soon."

Halfway down the path, Andi suddenly remembered the photo of the dachshund that she'd printed off the Internet. She'd meant to ask the Carters if it was related to their dogs. Glancing back, she saw that the front door was already closed.

Never mind, she thought. *I'll ask them next time.*

Natalie's mum ran Andi and Buddy back home just before nine o'clock that night. The Freestyling practice had gone so well that Andi had ended up staying to dinner so they could practise again afterwards. The only move Buddy still couldn't get the hang of was the sidestep that they'd learnt at their last class. It was a very advanced move but Andi was sure they'd get it right if they tried hard enough. Buddy was supposed to move to the side in a straight line, stepping with his back and front feet at the same time, but no matter how many times Andi showed him, he always moved his front feet first, then his back.

"How did the practice go?" Andi's mum called from the kitchen as Andi shut the front door.

"It was excellent! Buddy's doing really well, except for sidestepping. But even some of the dogs who've been going to classes for ages can't do that one yet."

"And Jet?"

"He's getting better, too."

"Do you want anything before bed?" Mrs Talbot asked.

"No thanks." Andi kissed her mum then headed upstairs. "Night, Mum."

"Night, darling. Sleep well." Buddy trotted after Andi.

When she was ready for bed, Andi snuggled down. Buddy settled in the crook of her legs with a contented sigh.

Andi shut her eyes, her head still full of the music she and Bud were using for their Freestyle dance. She pictured Buddy gazing up at her as he moved in time with the beat. She loved him so much, from his cute tan-and-white face right down to his paw with the missing claw. She loved the way he laid across her feet when she was working on the computer, and his habit of nudging her with his nose when he wanted to be stroked.

As she drifted into sleep, Andi's thoughts turned to Koko. The way he held her thumb with his tiny paws was so cute – and the way he wrinkled his nose and made his ears flap when he shook his head. It was a shame he'd been so sleepy after his trip to the clinic. Andi decided to have a word with Fisher and find out if that was normal.

In her mind's eye, she saw Koko lying sleepily on her lap, his velvety coat dark against her jeans. She imagined tracing her finger round the keyhole-shaped blotch on his tummy . . .

Andi sat bolt upright in bed. There hadn't been a keyhole-shaped patch on Koko's tummy today.

That wasn't Koko in Tooey's litter. It was a totally different puppy!

Chapter Seven

Andi leapt out of bed and raced downstairs. "Mum!" she yelled, bursting into the living room. "Something's happened to Koko!" She blurted out everything about going to the Carters' house and about how restless Tooey had seemed. "And Koko was so sleepy and not like his usual friendly self at all. And I've only just realized that's because it *wasn't him,*" she finished breathlessly.

Her mum looked stunned. "Are you sure, Andi?"

"Yes! He didn't do any of the things he usually did, and the keyhole-shaped patch on his tummy wasn't there. Tooey must have noticed it, too. That was why she was behaving so strangely." Andi ran a hand through her hair.

"Remember when you lost Buddy, Andi?" Mrs Talbot reminded her. "You followed another Jack Russell terrier that looked just like him. Perhaps two

84

of the Carters' puppies look alike and you picked up the wrong one."

"I didn't!" Andi insisted. "All the others have got cream patches. Koko is the only one who's dark all over."

Her mum frowned. "Well, the Carters know their own puppies! They'd have noticed if there was something wrong."

"But there *is* something wrong and they *haven't* noticed! Or they hadn't when I was there earlier." Andi could see why her mum didn't believe her – the whole thing sounded impossible – but she knew she was right. Somehow Koko had been switched!

"If you're really sure, you'll have to tell the Carters tomorrow," her mum said.

"Tomorrow? Oh, Mum, this can't wait!"

"It will have to. It's far too late to be phoning people now. And it's not as though they can do anything about it tonight."

"But, Mum . . ." Andi knew she'd never be able to sleep while she was worrying about Koko.

"No arguments, Andi. Back to bed now. You can speak to Mr and Mrs Carter in the morning."

Next morning, Andi met Natalie and Tristan on the corner of the Carters' road. She'd phoned the other

Pet Finders straight after breakfast to tell them about Koko and they'd decided it would be better to tell Shaun and Eleanor about Andi's suspicions face to face.

Andi had spent most of the night comparing the pup she'd named with the one she'd seen yesterday, and she was more certain than ever that they weren't the same. Having a jab might have made Koko less lively, but no way could it have changed his markings.

But just when she'd convinced herself that she was right about the switch, doubts crowded into her head. Just because she couldn't remember seeing the keyhole-shaped patch on Koko's tummy, did that mean it definitely wasn't there or had she simply not noticed it?

Andi's head ached from turning everything over and over.

"I'm not happy about having to do this," she confessed. "The Carters are going to be really shocked."

"You must have got it wrong," Tristan said. "How could anyone have switched one of the puppies? The Carters hardly let them out of their sight."

"I know. The whole thing seems impossible."

"If Andi thinks the puppy's not Koko, then she's probably right." Natalie defended her.

Tristan shrugged. "I still think we should have a look at the puppy before we say anything."

"Eleanor was rushing to get ready for a dinner party yesterday," Natalie remembered as they headed along the pavement. "She was really stressed about Zan Kirby coming over to look at Koko again." She stopped dead and stared at Andi and Tristan. "Hang on! Maybe she left Zan alone with the puppies. Perhaps *he* switched them!"

Andi was shocked. "But he seemed so nice!"

"Who else could it have been?" Natalie demanded. "And we know he liked Koko. Maybe he couldn't afford to pay for him, so he decided to steal him instead."

Andi frowned. "But where did the other puppy come from?"

"That's what we'll have to find out," Natalie said. "Come on!"

They reached the Carters' house and Tristan rang the doorbell. Andi was so nervous, she felt as though a tangle of worms was squirming in her stomach.

Shaun came to the door. He was wearing a pair of rubber gloves and carrying a wine glass that was dripping soapsuds on the carpet. "Hello," he said. "You're out early."

"Who is it, Shaun?" Eleanor called from the kitchen.

"It's Tooey's biggest fans!" joked Shaun. He opened the door wider. "Come in."

Andi felt herself going bright red as she stepped inside. What if she was wrong? The Carters were nice people and she didn't want to upset them for nothing.

Eleanor came out of the kitchen wearing a plastic apron. "I wasn't expecting to see you back so soon!" she said.

"I . . . um . . ." Andi stammered.

"Is something wrong with Buddy?" Shaun said, concerned.

Andi shook her head. "No. Buddy's fine. It's . . . It's one of the puppies. Koko. I only realized late last night."

"Realized what?" Eleanor prompted.

"I don't think he *is* Koko."

"What on earth do you mean?" Eleanor gasped.

"He's different," Andi ploughed on. "The keyhole patch on his tummy is missing. And yesterday he didn't do any of the things he usually does, like wrinkling his nose or flapping his ears or holding my thumb. He didn't even wag his tail." She looked desperately at Shaun and Eleanor. "I think he's been switched!"

Shaun darted into the living room. Eleanor followed him, snatching a photo of the puppies from the mantelpiece as she passed. Andi, Tristan and Natalie ran after her.

They all knelt round the dog basket. Shaun picked up the little chocolate-and-black puppy. "He looks like Koko to me," he said.

"But he's not behaving like Koko," Andi pointed out. The puppy was lying still in Shaun's hands. "Koko would have been squirming round and wagging his tail." Andi held out her thumb, but the puppy didn't make a grab for it. "Koko likes holding on to thumbs with his paws."

"Maybe he's still feeling woozy from his jab," Shaun suggested.

"Injections don't change the way puppies look," Andi persisted. She ran her fingers over the black patches on his back. Now she looked closely, she could see they were different to Koko's. "These patches are smaller than they should be. And look here." She took the puppy from Shaun and gently turned him over. "Koko has a keyhole-shaped patch on his tummy. But this puppy hasn't."

Eleanor held the photo next to the puppy. The picture showed Koko's tummy clearly.

There was a moment of tense silence, then Shaun said in a shocked voice: "You're right. This puppy's definitely not Koko."

"This puppy has a black stripe on his chest and Koko's chest is chocolate-brown," Tristan observed.

"And the tip of this pup's ear is brown, while Koko's ears are all black."

Andi didn't know whether to be relieved or horrified. She was glad they'd discovered the switch had been made, but she couldn't bear to think of poor Koko being separated from his mum and his brother and sisters.

Shaun sat back on his heels looking bewildered. "I don't understand. How could this have happened?"

"And why?" said Eleanor. "Why would someone steal a puppy and leave another one in its place? It doesn't make sense."

"Zan Kirby came here yesterday, didn't he?" said Tristan.

"That's right."

"Was he on his own with the puppies?" Andi asked.

"For a little while," Eleanor said. "Tooey seemed comfortable with him, and I was in such a rush to get ready for my dinner party."

"Can you remember anything odd about the way he looked?" Tristan prompted. "Did he bring anything with him, for example?"

"Only a rucksack. He said he was on his way to the gym."

"Was the rucksack big enough to hold a puppy?" Andi forced herself to ask. Koko would have been so frightened all alone in a stuffy gym bag!

The colour drained from Eleanor's face. "I suppose it was."

"How long was he with the puppies?" Natalie said.

"About five minutes."

"Long enough to do a switch, then," Tristan said grimly.

"He must have had this puppy in his bag when he arrived," Natalie said.

"There's something else, as well." Eleanor sank down on the arm of the sofa. "Not long after I'd left Zan with Tooey, I found him in the dining room at the back of the house. He said he was looking for the bathroom."

"Or a way out," Andi said grimly. "Maybe he thought Koko would bark and give him away if he didn't get out quickly."

Tristan began to pace up and down. "The thing we've got to work out is *why* Zan swapped the puppies. He obviously already had a dachshund puppy, so why would he bother to swap it for another one?"

"Perhaps he liked Koko better," Andi guessed. "Koko's livelier than this puppy. And he's funnier, too, with all those cute little habits."

"Livelier," Natalie echoed. "Maybe that's it. Maybe there's something wrong with this puppy, so he swapped it for your healthy one!"

Andi stared at her in dismay. However much she loved Koko, she didn't want there to be anything wrong with the substitute puppy!

They all waited anxiously while Shaun examined the puppy. It lay quietly in his lap while he checked its eyes, ears, teeth and fur. "I can't see anything obviously wrong with him," he said.

It was some consolation, but Andi was desperately worried about poor Koko. He could be anywhere if Zan had carried him off in his rucksack.

"What are we going to do?" Eleanor said. "This is the weirdest crime ever. It's lucky we've got the photos as proof."

"Can *we* look for Koko?" Natalie asked.

"Well, you can try!" said Shaun. "I've heard you Pet Finders are pretty successful. But we should still call the police."

"We could make posters," Andi began, then she shook her head. "There's no point. We already know tiny black-and-brown dachshund puppies look pretty much the same."

"We should investigate Zan Kirby," Tristan said. "Have you got an address or phone number for him?"

Shaun frowned. "We only corresponded with him by email."

"At least that means we've got his email address," Andi said.

"Come into the study." Eleanor Carter leapt up. "The computer's in there."

The Pet Finders followed her into the cosy room. Eleanor switched on the computer and brought up Zan's email. "Here's his first email."

Dear Mr and Mrs Carter,
I am interested in buying a miniature dachshund puppy. I have owned dachshunds before (see attached photos). I have visited your website many times and would be delighted to own one of your gorgeous puppies. Would it be possible to come and see the most recent litter, please?
Yours sincerely,
Zan Kirby.

Eleanor had shown the photos to the Pet Finders before, of a gorgeous dachshund with long black-and-tan fur and a smooth-coated fawn dachshund.

"The black-and-tan one looks really familiar," Andi said, frowning at the screen. She thought for a moment, and gasped. "Of course!" She fished in her rucksack and pulled out the photo she'd downloaded from the Internet. "Look!"

"It's the same dog!" Natalie exclaimed.

"Where did you get it?" Shaun asked.

"I downloaded it from a website."

Natalie looked confused. "What, Zan Kirby has a website?"

Andi shook her head. "I don't think so." She looked at the site details on the bottom of her printout. "There's nothing here about Kirby."

"Let's go to the website," Tristan suggested. "We need to find out if Zan really owned this dog."

The Pet Finders waited impatiently while Eleanor keyed in the address.

A colourful page, dotted with photos of miniature dachshunds, appeared on the screen.

"This is Emily Carr's website!" Shaun declared. "She's a top breeder!"

Eleanor pointed to a stunning image of a black-and-tan dog which took pride of place on the home page. It was the same dog as the one in Zan's picture. "There's no way Zan ever owned that dog," she said. "It's one of Emily's main breeding dogs."

"Zan Kirby must have downloaded the photo from the Internet to send to you. Which means he lied about owning dachshunds before," Natalie said. "He *must* have switched the puppies." She looked at Andi, her face pale with worry. "I hope we can find him before he does something bad to Koko."

"I don't think Zan will hurt him," Andi protested. But of course there was no way of knowing what Zan planned to do with the tiny puppy.

Eleanor clicked back to Zan's email, but it didn't contain his home address or his phone number.

"Can't we trace his personal details from his email?" Andi asked.

"It's a really complicated process," Tristan replied gloomily. "You have to have access to Internet service provider records. And I can't see any chance of us getting that."

"Well, we could send him an email asking him to get in touch," Andi persisted. She clicked the reply button and typed: *Please contact us urgently, Shaun and Eleanor Carter.*

"I shouldn't think he'll reply," Tristan warned darkly. "He won't want any more contact with you after what he's done."

Natalie sighed. "Good point. Right now, it looks as if Zan – and Koko – have vanished into thin air."

Chapter Eight

"I'm calling the police," announced Shaun Carter. Grim-faced, he dialled the number and switched on the phone's loudspeaker so everyone could hear.

A man answered the phone. "Sergeant Gray speaking. Can I help you?"

"I want to report a stolen puppy," Shaun told him.

"Yes, sir. Would you like to give me some details?"

The policeman listened while Shaun explained what had happened. When he'd finished, there was an awkward pause. "You don't think you could be mistaken, do you, sir? I mean, one puppy looks very like another."

"I know my own dogs, Sergeant," Shaun replied. "And I'm telling you that the puppies have been switched. I'm pretty sure I know who did it, too. A man called Zan Kirby."

"I see, sir. And why do you think this Zan Kirby would swap the puppies?"

"I don't know. But he was here yesterday and he had a bag with him big enough to hold a puppy."

The policeman took a deep breath. "Well, perhaps you'd like to take another look at the puppy and make sure it definitely isn't the one you think you've lost. To be honest, your lost puppy comes under the heading 'Missing Animals' so it isn't really a criminal matter."

"It is if he's been stolen," Shaun protested.

"But you still have the same number of puppies that you started out with," the policeman pointed out. "That sounds like rather an unusual thief to me. Look, sir, I don't mean to be unsympathetic but you have to admit this sounds very strange. Perhaps it would be best if you come down to the station to talk about it."

"I'll do that," said Shaun. He said goodbye and hung up.

"How rude!" Tristan burst out. "Imagine thinking you can't recognize your own puppy!"

Andi went back to the puppies' basket and crouched beside it. "I wonder where you came from," she mused, stroking the impostor's velvety head.

Tooey watched Andi with her head on one side. She had known all along the puppy wasn't hers. Andi rubbed her silky chest. "You're a good girl, Tooey. I need you to look after this poor little chap until we bring Koko home."

"Let's check the bucket!" Natalie yelled as soon as the bell rang for the start of school on Monday morning. She raced for the door with Tristan close behind her, but Andi got there first. She crossed her fingers for luck as she pelted along the corridor, hoping Cinnamon might have turned up.

To her disappointment, the catching bucket was still empty.

"Yet another impossible case for the Pet Finders," Natalie sighed.

"Cinnamon can't stay hidden for ever," Tristan pointed out.

"Perhaps we should organize a search of the whole school," Andi suggested. "Do you want me to speak to Mr Dixon about it?"

"Good idea," Tristan agreed.

The rest of the class came crowding in and news of Cinnamon's non-appearance began to spread. "I'd better get going," said Tristan. "Or Miss Ashworthy'll be on the warpath." He darted out of the room.

"I'll call Howard and give him an update," Andi said, noticing that he still wasn't back at school. "His teeth must be really bad. What on earth has he had done to them?"

As she took out her mobile phone, Natalie grabbed

her arm. "Wait! What if there isn't anything wrong with his teeth at all? What if Howard took Cinnamon home with him, and that's why he's staying away from school?"

Andi froze in the middle of calling up Howard's number. "Howard wouldn't do a thing like that, Nat."

"Listen. Cinnamon went missing last Thursday, right?" Natalie ticked off each point on her fingers. "Which was the day Howard left early to go to the dentist. Remember the way he went on about people not holding Cinnamon properly? Perhaps he decided Cinnamon shouldn't live at school any more. We don't know for sure that he even went to the dentist. That might have been the first excuse he could come up with for getting out of school before anyone discovered what he'd done." Natalie flipped her blonde hair back from her face. "If you ask me, he's staying at home because he doesn't want anyone to work out he stole Cinnamon!"

Andi realized Nat had a point. Howard had the opportunity and the motive for stealing Cinnamon. But Howard was kind-hearted and funny, and he'd never do anything to upset his friends. "I suppose he might have taken Cinnamon on impulse," she admitted. "But I'm still going to ring him. We need to talk to him."

She called his number.

Just as Howard's phone began to ring, Andi heard someone call her name: "Andi!"

She spun round. Howard was standing in the classroom doorway. Andi quickly switched off her phone. "Howard! Thank goodness you're here!"

Howard looked at her in surprise. "What's with the big welcome? I've only been gone a day and a half." His right cheek was red and swollen so he had obviously been telling the truth about having dental work done.

Andi and Natalie exchanged awkward glances. The evidence against Howard was starting to unravel. "I was worried about you, that's all," Andi said. "You sounded pretty bad when I phoned on Friday."

"Is there any news? Have you found Cinnamon?" Howard winced and pressed a hand to his cheek. "Ow, it still hurts to talk!"

"No, Cinnamon's not back yet," Andi told him. She watched his reaction closely, hating the fact she suspected another of her best friends of being a hamster thief.

Howard turned pale. "We should organize a search of the whole school," he said determinedly. "He's got to be somewhere. Come on, Andi. Let's talk to Mr Dixon about it."

Natalie opened her mouth to speak, but Andi shot her a look, warning her to keep quiet. Howard's dismay seemed totally genuine. He deserved an award if he was only acting. She was even more certain of his innocence when he sadly took a bag of sliced carrot from his rucksack and put it beside the empty cage.

"I wanted to give Cinnamon a treat to say welcome back," he sighed.

Andi took his arm. "Come on, let's go and talk to Mr Dixon about searching the whole school." She knew Howard would feel better if he was doing something positive to look for the missing hamster.

"It's a good idea," Mr Dixon said, when Andi and Howard told him their search plan. "Howard, you pop next door and ask Mrs Styles if her class could search. Is there anything in particular that they should be looking out for, Andi? You're a Pet Finder. I expect you know this sort of thing."

"Cinnamon would probably leave some nibbled paper about," Andi said. "And there might be a few gnaw marks on wooden furniture. And there'd be droppings, too."

"Right. Off you go then, Howard. You stay here, Andi, in case there are signs that Cinnamon's been in any of the classrooms. We'll need you and Natalie to go in there and try to follow his trail."

Mr Dixon sent people to each of the classes to ask their teachers to organize a search. Andi and Natalie waited anxiously, hoping for good news. Even a tiny tooth hole in a sheet of paper might give them the lead they so desperately needed.

One by one, the people Mr Dixon had sent to organize the searches came back. They all looked disappointed. Cinnamon was nowhere to be found.

"That's that, then," Andi said miserably, when Howard, the last to return, appeared in the doorway. "Cinnamon's nowhere." She sighed. It looked as though her worst fear had come true: Cinnamon must have got outside!

After school, Andi ran home to fetch Buddy for their Musical Freestyling class while Natalie and Tristan went to pick up Jet. They met up again outside the RSPCA centre. The car park was full and the lights were on in the windows. Natalie glanced at her watch and sighed. "Oh no! I've missed most of the Basic Obedience class."

"Never mind," Andi said. "At least we're in time for Freestyling."

Fisher's Obedience class was just ending when they went into the hall.

Andi, Natalie and Tristan sat down to wait for the

Musical Freestyling class to begin. Natalie picked up an animal magazine and began to flick through it, stopping at an article about animal rights.

Andi ruffled Buddy's ears and peered over Natalie's shoulder. "Look at this!" she exclaimed. "This article is written by Alexander Kirby!"

Tristan raised his eyebrows. "So?" Then he sat up straighter. "Oh, do you think he could be related to the Kirby who took Koko?"

"No! I think he might be the *same* person! Think about it. Zan could be short for Alexander!"

"Oh my goodness! You might be right," Natalie said.

"And if he's an *animal* journalist," Andi continued excitedly, "then it's pretty likely he'd be able to get his hands on another puppy to make the switch."

"Andi, you're a genius!" Tristan declared.

"Don't tell her that," Natalie told him. "She'll only get big-headed!"

Buddy and Jet picked up on their excitement and began to bark. "Shush, Buddy," Andi said. She glanced round the hall, looking for Shaun Carter: she couldn't wait to tell him about the article! To her disappointment, he and Whisper hadn't arrived yet.

"Let's write down the name of this magazine," Natalie said.

Tristan fished his red notebook out of his rucksack

and wrote down the title – *Animal Matters* – along with the address and phone number. "We should give them a ring tomorrow and ask to speak to Alexander Kirby. He's got a lot of explaining to do."

Chloe arrived and the lesson began, though Shaun still hadn't turned up. Andi found it really hard to concentrate. Twice she nearly trod on Buddy's toes because she kept looking at the door, hoping to see Shaun coming in.

"Is something wrong, Andi?" Chloe asked.

"I was just wondering where Shaun Carter had got to. I wanted to speak to him."

"He's not coming this evening. Eleanor rang me earlier to say he had to work late."

"Oh, right." Andi felt a stab of disappointment, then reminded herself that the Pet Finders couldn't do anything about tracking the journalist down tonight because the magazine office would be closed.

"Sorry, Bud." She rubbed the top of Buddy's head. "I promise I'll watch what I'm doing from now on."

Buddy pricked up his ears as though he was listening to the music. Andi raised her hand and they began to back across the hall.

At lunchtime next day, the Pet Finders met up in the school playground to phone *Animal Matters*. Tristan recited the number without looking it up in his notebook.

"I wish I had a memory like yours," Natalie sighed.

Tristan grinned. "Some of us have it and some of us don't!"

Natalie dialled the number. "I'll use speakerphone, then we can all hear what Alexander 'Zan' Kirby has to say."

The phone was answered almost at once. "*Animal Matters*," said a woman's voice.

"Oh, hello. Can I speak to Alexander Kirby, please?" said Natalie. "I read what he wrote about animal rights and I've got a good idea for a follow-up article."

"I'm afraid Mr Kirby is out of the office at the moment, but if you'd like to leave a message I'll pass it on to him when he gets back from the book-signing."

Natalie gave her mobile number, then switched off the phone. "I hope he rings."

"How many book-signings are likely to be going on in Aldcliffe today?" Andi asked.

Tristan shrugged. "I don't know. Not too many."

Andi punched the air. "Then I bet we can go and talk to Alexander Kirby in person! He's going to be at Reeder's bookshop."

Tristan's mouth dropped open. "How do you know?"

"Andi's psychic," Natalie said in a spooky voice.

"Don't forget she was the one who sensed that Koko had been switched."

"We saw posters about a signing in Reeder's window," Andi explained. "Dale Savage is coming to promote his latest book. It's exactly the sort of thing that would appeal to *Animal Matters* readers." She pulled out her phone. "I'll ring Shaun and Eleanor to tell them that we've tracked down Zan Kirby and that we're hoping to speak to him this afternoon."

"Good idea!" said Tristan. "Alexander Kirby is going to have some *very* tricky questions to answer!"

Chapter Nine

The Pet Finders dashed out of school the moment the bell rang at the end of the day. Andi could hardly wait to get to the bookshop. Surely they must be getting close to finding Koko now!

As they headed for the gate, Tanya McLennan brushed past, not even slowing down to say goodbye.

"Hamster cage!" Tristan exclaimed, stopping dead in the middle of the pavement.

Andi and Natalie stared at him. "What are you on about, Tris?" Andi asked.

"Tanya's got a hamster cage. Don't you remember, we delivered it for Mike."

Andi frowned. "So? She said it was for a mouse."

"She *said* it was for a mouse," Tristan agreed, with heavy emphasis. "But what if it was for a hamster? One hamster in particular . . ."

Andi's head spun. Were they going to end up

suspecting everyone in their class of stealing Cinnamon?

"Let's go and talk to her." Natalie shot off along the pavement, where Tanya was just opening a car door.

"Wait, Tanya!" Andi yelled, sprinting past Natalie.

Tanya glanced round, startled. "Oh hi, Andi."

"That hamster cage we delivered," Andi panted, skidding to a halt beside Tanya.

"What about it?"

Andi thought fast. She could hardly accuse Tanya of stealing Cinnamon just because she'd taken delivery of a hamster cage. "I . . . I was just wondering whether you could bring your mouse to school. The smell of another small rodent might attract Cinnamon back to the classroom."

"Sorry, I still haven't got the mouse yet." Tanya opened the car door and climbed inside. "Sorry I can't help," she called through the window as her mum drove away.

"Could you really keep a mouse in a hamster cage?" Natalie said.

Tristan shrugged. "Probably. They're about the same size."

"But it's weird to order a *hamster* cage if it's for a mouse," Natalie persisted. "It's like asking for a small dog's bed when you want a place for your cat to sleep."

"That's true," Andi said. "This is starting to look pretty suspicious."

Natalie nodded. "I think we need to talk to Tanya again – fast!"

"What about the book-signing?" Tristan said. "We don't want to miss Zan Kirby."

"It doesn't end until five o'clock," Andi said, remembering the poster in the bookshop window. "There'll be time to talk to Tanya first." She set off at a run.

"Hang about!" Tristan called after her.

Andi skidded to a halt and looked back impatiently. "Come on! There's no time to waste."

"Let's catch the bus!" Tristan said. He and Natalie darted across the road to where a bus was just pulling up. "It'll be quicker than running – and a lot less exhausting!"

Andi raced back and jumped on to the bus as well.

They sat on the long back seat. "It wouldn't have taken long to run to Tanya's house," Andi pointed out. "It's probably only a couple of stops. And I've been so busy with Freestyling and puppies that I haven't been for a run for ages."

"Nat and I might be getting fitter thanks to your energetic approach to finding pets," said Tristan, "but we don't want to wear our feet out completely!"

"Definitely," Natalie agreed. She took out a compact mirror and checked her reflection. "Anyway, running messes my hair up." She pushed a strand of hair behind her ear and put the mirror away again.

"Of course, Nat. You can't possibly let Tanya see you with messed-up hair," Andi teased. She caught sight of her own reflection in the bus window and broke off. Her own hair was sticking up all over! "You could have told me!" she protested.

"I thought that was the look you wanted," Natalie replied innocently. "The 'I've just been running' look."

"If you two could stop discussing hairstyles for two seconds," Tristan cut in, "you might notice that we need to get off."

The bus stopped at the end of Tanya's street. Her mum's car was parked on the drive. "Good, they're home already," said Andi.

"What are we going to say to her?" Tristan asked as he rang the bell.

"Perhaps you could tell her Christine's got some mice for sale, Tris," Andi suggested.

"Or we could just ask her straight out if she knows anything about Cinnamon's disappearance," said Natalie.

Suddenly the door opened and Tanya's little sister, Marie, appeared on the step. "Hello," she said.

Andi stared at her in astonishment. Marie was holding Cinnamon!

"Look at my hamster!" said Marie, holding Cinnamon up proudly. "Tanya gave him to me for my birthday."

Andi was speechless. Tanya had stolen Cinnamon for her sister's birthday present!

"He's beautiful," Tristan said in a strained voice. "Is Tanya in, Marie?"

Tanya came out of a door in the hallway. She went bright red when she saw the Pet Finders. "You'd better come in," she mumbled. "Marie, go and put your hamster in his cage."

Andi, Natalie and Tristan followed Tanya upstairs to her bedroom. Andi could hardly believe what was happening: one of their classmates *was* a thief after all!

"How could you, Tanya?" Natalie burst out as soon as the bedroom door was closed. "You stole Cinnamon!"

Tanya hung her head. "I know it was wrong, but I wanted to get Marie a really memorable birthday present. She's been so ill. I thought she deserved something special."

"Oh, yes! A stolen hamster is really memorable!" Natalie said.

"You could have *bought* a hamster at Paws for Thought," Tristan pointed out.

114

"I know. And I did look at hamsters in the pet shop, but Marie's favourite colour is orange and they didn't have any hamsters that colour. I knew Cinnamon would be perfect."

"Our whole class has been worried sick!" Andi said. "Didn't you care?" She could see that Tanya was upset, but she deserved to feel bad after what she'd done.

"I didn't think anyone would be that bothered when I took Cinnamon," Tanya said in a quavery voice. "I thought we'd just get a new hamster to replace him." Her eyes filled with tears. "It was awful when I saw how upset everyone was, but it was too late to own up by then. You'd all have been mad at me."

"We *are* mad at you!" Natalie snapped. "Cinnamon doesn't belong to you."

"I know! I wish I could turn everything back to how it was, but I can't." Tanya threw herself down on the bed and buried her face in her pillow. "I only did it for Marie."

Andi couldn't help feeling sorry for her. "What are we going to do?" she whispered to Tristan and Natalie. "Tanya's going to be in monster trouble at school when this comes out."

"Good!" Natalie said.

"I know it was wrong," Tanya sobbed, sitting up.

"And I promise I'll never do anything like this again. Not ever!"

"We should help her, Nat," Andi said. "She's learnt her lesson."

Natalie shrugged. "OK. If you've got a plan to sort things out, I'm listening."

"Me too," said Tristan.

"What's going to happen now?" Tanya asked tearfully.

Andi sat beside Tanya on the bed. "First, you've got to tell your mum where Cinnamon really came from."

Tanya gulped. "She'll be furious!"

"If you don't tell her, we will," Natalie warned. "And it would sound better coming from you."

"But we'll tell Marie, if you like," Andi offered. She knew Tanya was going to find it hard enough confessing the truth to her mum.

Tanya nodded. "Thanks." She stood up and dried her eyes. "I'll go and get Marie; then I'll speak to Mum."

A few moments later, Marie came in looking puzzled. "Tanya said you wanted to tell me something."

"That's right," Tristan said gently. "I don't think you're going to like it much, Marie."

Marie's eyes widened. She picked at a *HAPPY BIRTHDAY 5 TODAY* badge pinned to her sweatshirt and Andi realized it was actually her birthday that day. That made everything a hundred times worse!

"When Tanya gave you Cinnamon, she wanted you to have a really special present," Andi began. "The trouble is, Cinnamon already belonged to somebody else."

Marie's bottom lip quivered. "Someone else? Is the person sad because they haven't got a hamster any more?"

"Cinnamon belongs to lots of people," Andi said. "And they all miss him very much."

Marie gasped. "Do they want him back?"

"Yes, they do," Andi replied. "You see, they didn't mean Tanya to take Cinnamon in the first place." She glanced at the others, hoping they agreed with her decision to avoid talking about theft and stealing. Natalie gave her an encouraging nod.

"So it was a mistake?" Marie checked.

"That's right," said Andi. "Cinnamon can't be your pet because he still belongs to these other people."

"But you can choose a new hamster from the pet shop," said Tristan, "and it will be just as lovable as Cinnamon."

Marie gazed at them in dismay. "But Cinnamon is *my* hamster. I was going to teach him some tricks."

"You can teach your new hamster tricks," Natalie

promised. "And if you choose it yourself, you'll be able to pick the one with the prettiest colour."

Marie nodded hesitantly. "I suppose so."

"And Cinnamon belongs to our class, so you can come in and see him when you come to meet Tanya from school," Andi told her.

Marie looked a bit more cheerful. "I'd like that. Then I'll sort of have two hamsters – one at home and one at school. I'll go and tell him." She went out of the room.

Tristan rubbed his hands over his face. "Phew, I'm glad that's over."

"Me, too," said Natalie. "It's good that we've got Cinnamon back, but I feel so sorry for Marie. None of this is her fault."

"Come on," Andi said heavily. "We can't stay up here."

They trooped downstairs. As they reached the bottom, Tanya and Mrs McLennan came out of the kitchen. Tanya's eyes were red-rimmed, and her mum looked angry.

"Tanya's told me all about Cinnamon," said Mrs McLennan. "I'll tell Marie to bring him down."

"I've got a shoebox in my room," Tanya said. "We could put Cinnamon in there." She hurried upstairs to fetch it.

Mrs McLennan tried to smile at the Pet Finders.

"I'm so sorry Tanya has caused all this trouble."

"Please don't worry, Mrs McLennan," said Tristan. "The main thing is we've found Cinnamon safe and sound."

Marie came downstairs, carrying Cinnamon in her hands. "You've got to go back to your real owners," she whispered, looking tearful.

Tanya appeared behind her with the shoebox. She had made some holes in the lid so that Cinnamon would be able to breathe, and she'd put plenty of shredded-paper bedding inside to keep him warm.

Marie gulped. "You'll like it at school, Cinnamon," she said. "I'll come and see you lots, I promise." She placed him gently in the box and Tanya put on the lid.

Tristan took out his mobile phone. "I'll ring Christine Wilson, the owner of Paws for Thought, to see if she's got any orange hamsters."

"Can I give Cinnamon a lettuce leaf, Mum?" Tanya asked.

"Of course you can, darling," said Mrs McLennan.

Tanya fetched a leaf from the fridge. As she slipped it into the box, Andi heard her whisper, "Sorry, Cinnamon."

"Christine's got a new litter of hamsters and some of them have tan markings," Tristan announced, switching off his mobile.

"That's good news," Mrs McLennan said. "Do you hear that, Marie? We can go and choose a new hamster straight away."

Marie smiled.

"We'd better go," Andi said. She picked up the box and carried it carefully out of the house. Natalie and Tristan followed her.

As they walked down the drive, Tanya ran after them. "Wait! What about school? Are you going to tell everyone that I stole Cinnamon?"

Andi looked at Tristan and Natalie.

Tristan shrugged. "The main thing is that Cinnamon will be back where he belongs."

"Nat?" Andi prompted.

Natalie looked thoughtful. "I suppose we could put Cinnamon in the catching bucket early in the morning, so it will look as if he made his own way back."

Andi nodded. "Yes, that sounds like a good idea."

"Thank you so much!" Tanya gasped. "I promise I'll never steal anything again."

Looking at her pale, anxious face, Andi believed her completely.

Chapter Ten

There was no time to take Cinnamon home, so Andi tucked the box inside her jacket to shield the little hamster from the chilly wind. Then they walked to the bookshop – Andi couldn't run because Cinnamon would have been jolted about.

"I hope we're still in time," Tristan said as they turned into Main Street.

Luckily the bookshop was still packed with people listening to Dale Savage read a chapter from his book. He was a suntanned man, aged about thirty, with collar-length blond hair and a mischievous grin. About fifty people were sitting on chairs and almost that many again were standing at the back and sides of the shop. Andi, Natalie and Tristan squeezed into a tiny gap just inside the door.

"Can you see him?" Andi asked, stretching up on tiptoe and craning her neck to see past the people in front of her.

"Over there," a lady said kindly, pointing to Dale Savage. "I'm surprised you don't recognize him from TV."

"Oh, yeah, thanks," Andi said, trying not to giggle. She wasn't looking for Dale Savage!

"Look, there!" Natalie said in a low voice, pointing across the room. Right at the back, standing on a chair and taking notes, was a familiar red-haired figure. Zan Kirby!

"Come on!" Tristan whispered. He began to push through the crowd, trying to reach the journalist.

"What do you think you're doing?" a man hissed. "These seats are taken. You'll have to stand."

"I don't want to sit down," Tristan whispered, going red. "I want to speak to someone over there."

"You'll have to wait until there's more space!" the man told him.

"Come back, Tris," Andi said, pulling him away. "If we stay near the door, Zan can't leave until we've talked to him."

Dale Savage was still reading: "The most important thing is that dogs recognize you as pack leader. If your dog is lying on the chair you want to sit on, make him get up and move. It might seem mean, but your dog will love you for it in the end because he'll understand that he's part of your pack, not the other way round." He closed his book. "Does anyone have any questions?"

Tristan's hand shot up.

"Yes, over there?" said Dale.

"Come through to the front so Dale can see you," said a lady wearing a pink jacket.

"I hope he's not going to do anything stupid," Natalie said to Andi, as Tristan wriggled to the front of the crush.

Tristan stood beside Dale and pointed dramatically at Zan Kirby. "Actually, I want to speak to that journalist over there. We know what you did to the Carters!"

Everyone turned to stare at Zan. The colour drained from his face and he stared at Tristan in dismay.

"I ... I ..." He stepped down from his chair, looking startled. "Listen, let's go outside and talk about this," he called. "I can explain everything," he told the people round him.

Andi watched Zan push his way towards the door. It was taking him so long she was afraid he'd have time to think up a plausible story to convince them he hadn't swapped the puppies.

The man who'd moaned at Tristan blocked Zan's way. "We've come here to listen to Dale, not watch you and this boy sort out your personal problems."

"Sorry," Zan said. "But I just want to get past . . ."

The man shifted reluctantly and Zan reached the door. He looked even more startled to see Andi and Natalie waiting for him. He obviously recognized them.

Tristan came over, his hair sticking on end. "Well?" he demanded.

Zan Kirby shook his head. "I'll tell you everything, but not here where everyone can listen."

"We can talk outside," Andi said. She didn't want to give Zan any longer to think up a good story.

They went outside. A cold wind was blowing and Andi pulled her jacket more tightly around the shoebox, remembering what Tristan had said about hamsters needing warmth.

Natalie turned to face Zan as soon as they reached the pavement. "You never meant to buy one of the Carters' puppies, did you? You just wanted to switch your puppy with Koko."

"Switch puppies? What do you mean?" Zan looked bewildered.

"Were you planning to buy one of their puppies?" Natalie prompted.

Zan looked uncomfortable. "Well, not exactly."

"I knew it!"

"But I still don't know anything about switching puppies," Zan insisted. He glanced round, then lowered his voice. "Look, I'm an investigative journalist and I'm writing an article about puppy farms. I've been pretending to be a prospective buyer so I can investigate breeders."

"But the Carters look after their dogs really well," Andi protested. "You don't have to investigate them!"

Zan nodded impatiently. "I know that now. I visited them twice because they seemed too good to be true and I wanted to check their total set-up, not just the bits they wanted me to see." He fished in his bag and took out a dictaphone. "Listen. This will prove it." He switched it on and they heard his voice, speaking quietly: "Mother dog in good health. Eyes and teeth clean. Coat good condition. Fresh water available." He switched it off. "OK?"

Andi had to admit it looked as though he was telling the truth. "So you really don't know anything about the switch?"

"What switch?"

"Koko, the black-and-chocolate puppy that you liked best, has been swapped for a puppy from another litter," she told him.

Zan's eyes lit up and Andi remembered he was a journalist. This was the sort of scoop that his readers would love! "Why would anyone do a thing like that?" he said.

"We're not sure," Andi admitted.

"We also don't know how," said Natalie. "The puppies haven't been alone with anyone except you."

Zan grinned unexpectedly. "In that case, I can see how you thought I was the culprit. Good detective work, tracking me down like that!"

"We're the Pet Finders Club," Andi explained.

"The Pet Finders Club?" Zan echoed.

"Yup," Tristan said. "We do stuff like this all the time. But this is one of our trickier cases."

Zan took out his notebook. "I think there's a story here. Can I cover it for *Animal Matters*?"

"It's OK with us, but you'd have to ask the Carters," Tristan said. He looked at Andi and Natalie. "And it looks like we're going to have to do a lot more detective work to solve this case."

"Let me know if I can help in any way," said Zan.

"Thanks," Tristan said. "Good luck with investigating the puppy farms."

"We should tell the Carters that it wasn't Zan who took Koko," Andi said, when Zan had gone back into the bookshop. She lifted the lid of the shoebox to check that Cinnamon was all right; he was curled up in the middle of the shredded paper, fast asleep.

"We must be missing something," Natalie sighed as they set off towards the Carters' house. "The puppies must have been left on their own with someone else."

"Hang on!" Andi exclaimed, stopping so suddenly that Tristan almost walked into her. "Eleanor took Tooey and the puppies to Mr Harvey's vet's clinic the day Koko went missing. She said it looked as though every puppy in town was there having jabs."

"Perhaps the nurse muddled up two litters while she was putting them back in their baskets," Natalie said excitedly.

Andi handed Cinnamon to Tristan and took out her mobile phone. "I'll ring the Carters and find out if that could have happened. Then we can go straight over to the clinic."

Eleanor Carter answered the phone.

"Hello, it's Andi. Zan Kirby definitely didn't switch the puppies."

"How do you know?"

"We've spoken to him. He's a journalist and he was doing an undercover investigation into puppy-farming."

Eleanor gasped.

"It's OK," Andi said quickly. "He really liked the way you do things and he knows you're great breeders. But we just remembered that you took the puppies to the vet's that day. Were you with the puppies the whole time?"

There was a pause from Eleanor before she replied. "I left them at the clinic for a few minutes while I popped to the shop across the street. I had to buy some cream for the dinner party. But Mr Harvey is very reliable. He would never have allowed puppies to be switched."

"It might have happened by accident," Andi said. "Perhaps there was another litter of miniature dachshunds having jabs at the same time. We'll go to the vet's now and find out. Thanks, Eleanor." She hung up quickly.

"Well?" Tristan demanded.

Andi held up her crossed fingers. "The vet's, quick! It looks like we've got a new lead."

Mr Harvey, a tall man with grey hair and kind eyes, was in the waiting room, chatting to Teresa, the veterinary nurse, when the Pet Finders burst in. "What's the emergency?" he joked.

"We're investigating a missing-puppy case," Tristan puffed.

"It's Koko, one of the Carters' puppies," Natalie added.

Mr Harvey frowned. "Koko's missing! Poor Shaun and Eleanor! They must be so worried."

"The thing is," Andi continued, "Koko was

switched for another puppy and we think it might have happened here. By mistake," she added hastily, as the nurse looked horrified.

"That's impossible," Teresa said. She was wearing dog-shaped earrings, and a silver cat brooch was pinned to the collar of her white uniform. "Puppies stay in their carriers until they're in the consulting room. The Carters' puppies couldn't possibly have been muddled up with another litter."

"Well, then, if it didn't happen by accident," Natalie said, "someone must have deliberately switched the puppies."

"But why would anyone do that?" Teresa asked.

"I don't know, but I think I know how they did it!" Tristan declared. "It's like that old story about stealing a wheelbarrow from a building site. The guard will let you through when he sees the wheelbarrow is empty."

"What are you talking about, Tris?" Natalie said. "We're looking for a puppy, not a wheelbarrow."

"But it's the same thing, don't you see? Nobody would have thought anything was strange if someone brought in a puppy." Tristan turned to Teresa. "Could you check your records and see if anyone else brought a miniature dachshund in that day?"

"There *was* another miniature dachshund," she agreed. "I remember him. A sweet little thing." She flipped over a couple of pages in the appointment book. "Here we are. The puppy belonged to someone called Mr Lance Sinden. It was his first visit."

"He must have come just to switch the puppies!" said Tristan.

"So we know who might have done it, and how," Andi said. "But we still don't know why."

"We thought there might have been something wrong with the puppy that was left in Koko's place," Natalie told Mr Harvey. "But Shaun Carter thought he looked OK."

Mr Harvey frowned. "It's not always that straightforward. Sometimes puppies suffer from inherited disorders that only show up after tests. For example, acanthosis nigricans is a common skin complaint in dachshunds, and that won't show until a pup's about three months old. An eye disorder called corneal dystrophy can affect dachshunds, too."

"So the puppy could be ill after all?" Andi gasped.

"Possibly. We need to give him a check-up," Mr Harvey replied. "I'll call Shaun and Eleanor and ask them to bring him in. And it's vital to track down his owner because he could know exactly what's wrong with him."

"Can we have Mr Sinden's address?" Natalie asked.

"I'm sorry," Mr Harvey said. "We can't give out

addresses because of patient confidentiality." He looked as if he was about to say something else, but just then a flustered lady rushed in, looking very red in the face and staggering under the weight of a heavy pet carrier. Mr Harvey and the nurse went to help her, leaving the Pet Finders standing by the counter.

"I think we should go," said Natalie. "We aren't going to get Lance Sinden's address from here."

"Perhaps he's in the phone book," Andi said. "We could go back to your house, Nat, and look him up."

She and Nat held the door open for Tristan, who walked slowly, holding Cinnamon's box level.

"It's funny," Andi said once they were outside. "I feel as though I've heard of Lance Sinden, but I can't think where."

They headed for Natalie's house, weaving their way carefully between last-minute shoppers in the high street so Cinnamon wouldn't be bumped about.

Suddenly Tristan gave a shout. "Yes!"

"What? Have you thought of something?" Andi asked eagerly.

"There's the Banana Beach Café. Why don't we talk about the case there, over a slice of cake? I'm sure we could borrow their phone book."

"That's it!" Andi whooped.

"What's it?" Natalie asked, puzzled.

"I've just remembered where I've heard Lance Sinden's name before. Remember those cakes that were sent to school, just before Cinnamon went missing? Lance Sinden is the new pastry chef at the Treetops Hotel!"

Chapter Eleven

Andi phoned Shaun Carter that night to tell him what they'd found out. "I've never heard of Lance Sinden in dog-breeding circles," he said, "but if he is the thief, I don't want you going anywhere near him on your own." "Natalie's reserved a table for us at the hotel for tea tomorrow," Andi said. "But we're only going to check the place out and see if we can spot Koko. We're not planning to speak to Lance Sinden."

"I'm free tomorrow. Why don't I come with you?"

"That would be perfect!"

"OK. What time are you going?"

"Five o'clock. That gives us time to change after school." Andi paused. "And, er . . . Natalie thinks we need to look nice or the hotel won't let us in." She hoped Shaun wouldn't be offended, but she'd only ever seen him wearing faded dog-friendly jeans and an old sweatshirt.

"Don't worry, I'll dress up for the occasion," Shaun said good-humouredly.

"We'll meet you there, then," Andi said.

Next morning, Natalie brought Cinnamon to school in the shoebox. "Is he OK?" Andi asked.

Natalie glanced round to make sure no one was watching them, then lifted the lid. Cinnamon looked up at Andi, his beady eyes looking bright and curious as he nibbled a sunflower seed held between his front paws.

"He's so cute," Andi sighed. "Everyone will be really happy to have him back."

"We're going to have to sneak him inside before the bell goes," said Tristan. He made a face. "Let's hope Miss Ashworthy's not on the prowl."

They hurried to the main door but there were two teachers talking in the entrance hall. "Let's try round the side," Andi suggested. There was a fire escape door near the classroom; the caretaker sometimes left it propped open when he was working outside.

To the Pet Finders' relief, the side door was open. The caretaker was unblocking a drain nearby. He was kneeling down with his back to them, pushing a rod into the drain.

"We'll have to be quiet," Natalie whispered.

They crept towards the door. Andi's heart thudded so hard it was a wonder the whole school didn't hear it. If they were caught, it would wreck their plan to sneak Cinnamon inside without anyone finding out what had really happened.

Luckily the caretaker was humming to himself and he didn't hear them sneak past. Keeping a wary eye out for teachers, they tiptoed along the corridor.

Suddenly they heard footsteps heading their way. "In here, quick!" Tristan gasped, flinging open a door. They squeezed into the cramped cupboard and Tristan pulled the door shut, plunging them into darkness.

"Can you move over a bit, Andi?" Natalie hissed. "I've got a broom handle digging into my back."

"Sorry. I haven't got much space either. My face is squished against a can of furniture polish." The smell was making Andi's eyes water, and she tried hard not to sneeze.

"Shh," Tristan warned.

The footsteps passed by outside. "Stay here," Tristan whispered. "I'll see if the coast's clear."

He cautiously opened the door and looked out. "So far so good."

Andi watched him tiptoe along the corridor. At the corner, he stopped and looked back, then beckoned them forward.

"Come on, Nat." Andi felt an urge to giggle. "It feels like we're in a spy film!"

They reached the classroom without meeting any teachers, and Natalie lifted the hamster out of the shoebox and placed him in the catching bucket. "There," she said. "Nobody will ever guess he wasn't in the school the whole time."

She was interrupted by the bell ringing for the start of school.

"Quick!" said Andi. "We don't want anyone to find us in here!"

Natalie stuffed the shoebox in her rucksack, then they scurried out of the classroom and along the corridor, heading towards the main entrance. As soon as they saw people hurrying to class, they turned and sauntered back the way they had come, as if they'd been first into school. Andi and Natalie took their time over hanging their coats on the pegs outside the classroom to give someone else a chance to discover Cinnamon. As Nat had said, the person to find the body was usually the culprit!

By the time they went into the classroom, an excited crowd had gathered round the catching bucket.

"Andi, he's back!" Howard called. "The catching bucket worked!"

Andi, Natalie and Tristan hurried over. "That's brilliant!" Andi exclaimed. And she meant it too; she was so glad to have the little hamster back.

Howard lifted Cinnamon out of the bucket and looked him over. "He's obviously been eating OK since he went missing. He doesn't look thin or anything." He ran his finger over the hamster's head. "I'm glad you're back, boy."

Cinnamon sat up on Howard's hand, his nose quivering, and cleaned his face with his tiny paws.

"Let's get you back in your cage," Howard said. "Can you open the door for me, Larissa?"

"OK. And I'll get him some fresh bedding." Larissa touched Cinnamon's head with one finger. The hamster went on washing his face. Larissa stroked him gently, her face breaking into a smile. "His fur's so soft," she breathed. "I don't know why I was scared of him."

Tanya came into class. She stopped in the doorway and looked warily at Andi and Natalie.

"Hey, Tanya," Howard called. "We've got Cinnamon back. The catching bucket worked!"

"That's great, Howard," said Tanya. "I'm really happy." As she passed Andi, she whispered, "Thanks."

"Has Marie chosen a new hamster?" Andi asked in a low voice.

"Yeah. A cute little golden one." Tanya smiled. "She

wanted to call it Cinnamon, but Mum persuaded her that Spice would be a better name. I think one Cinnamon is enough!"

When the Pet Finders arrived at the hotel just before five o'clock, Andi was surprised at how smart the lobby was. The floor was pink-veined marble and huge marble pillars supported the high ceiling. An immaculately-dressed lady stood at the reception counter beside a leather suitcase.

"Wow! This place is sooo smart," Andi whispered.

Natalie looked surprised. "Do you think so? My mum and I always have tea in hotels like this after we've been shopping."

A porter in a blue uniform and peaked cap directed them to the dining room. All of the hotel staff were wearing bow ties, and the head waiter addressed Natalie as "Miss Lewis'.

Shaun was waiting for them at their table, wearing a button-down shirt and a tie; a pale linen jacket was slung over the back of his chair. "They let me in," he joked, "so I must look nice enough." Then he became more serious. "I took the impostor puppy to Mr Harvey today. He'll need to do some tests to check all the possibilities unless his real owner can be found."

"So that's two puppies in peril," Andi said. "Let's hope this lead takes us somewhere."

"And while we're waiting to find out more about Lance Sinden," Tristan said, "we might as well have some food. I'm starving."

"I've already ordered a selection of finger sandwiches," Shaun said. "Is that all right?"

"That's wonderful," Andi said, smoothing down her wool skirt. "Thank you very much."

"Yes, thank you!" chimed in Tristan and Natalie.

Andi looked round the dining room. It had a high ornate ceiling, walls covered in rich red wallpaper and a carpet so soft and thick that the waiters' feet made no noise at all. The high-backed chairs were gold-painted with red padded seats, the tables were covered with crisp white cloths, and the china was so fine Andi could practically see through it. A silver knife and a cake fork lay beside each plate.

"This must be what it's like to have tea with the Queen," Tristan whispered.

A smartly-dressed waiter brought a tray of sandwiches to their table. Another brought a jug of orange juice.

Shaun thanked them. "So what's the plan?" he asked when the waiters were out of earshot.

"We're going to ask if we can speak to the new

pastry chef," Tristan explained. "And when Lance Sinden appears, we'll confront him about the puppy switch." He took a sandwich.

A waiter came over. "Is everything to your satisfaction?"

"Yes, wonderful, thank you," Natalie said politely.

"Really nice!" Andi agreed. She took a deep breath. This was their chance! "Could I speak to the new pastry chef? He sent some lovely cakes to my class a little while ago, and I'd like to say thank you in person."

The waiter smiled. "Lance would be really pleased to meet you, Miss, but he only works in the mornings."

"Oh no!" Tristan exclaimed. "I want to be a pastry chef when I grow up and I was hoping he could give me some career advice."

"Well, you could always pop in and see him one morning," the waiter suggested.

Tristan swallowed the last of his sandwich and stood up. "Thanks very much. I'll do that."

Shaun paid the bill and they went out of the hotel. "That was bad luck. Perhaps we should book a table for morning coffee."

"We'd have to wait till Saturday," Andi groaned. "And poor Koko . . ." She broke off and gripped Natalie's arm. "Look!" She pointed to a pair of wide-legged checked trousers and a white jacket that were hanging on a washing line at the side of a long, two-storey block of flats. "That's the sort of uniform a chef wears. Perhaps it belongs to Lance Sinden."

"He'd have to live close to the hotel," Natalie agreed. "Pastry chefs start work really early. My mum's friend is married to a pastry chef and he sometimes starts work at three o'clock in the morning."

"I wonder if his name's on his uniform," Tristan said. "Shall we go and see?"

They jogged along the driveway that ran between the hotel and the block of flats. "You three are amazing," said Shaun, running beside them. "You never give up!"

As they stopped beside the washing line, a rather tatty car came along the drive and stopped in front of the apartments. A tall woman wearing an old-fashioned windcheater and a headscarf decorated with dogs climbed out.

"That's Stella Milton!" Shaun exclaimed. "She breeds miniature dachshunds too."

"What a coincidence, to meet a friend here," Andi remarked.

"Oh, Stella's not really a friend," Shaun admitted. "More of a show rival, really!" He grinned. "Her dogs are hot competition for Tooey and Snowy." He raised his voice. "Hello, Stella. This is a surprise."

The woman turned round. "Shaun!" she gasped. "How nice to see you!"

"Did you hear, Tooey's had her pups?" Shaun said. "Four girls and—"

Stella Milton didn't let him finish. "Yes, yes. I saw them on your website." She looked round. "Oh dear, I seem to have come to the wrong place. Excuse me!" She hurried back to her car.

Just then, a young man with curly brown hair looked out of a first-floor window. "Hey, Aunt Stella! Where are you going?"

For a moment, Stella didn't move. Then she slammed her car door again and locked it. She smiled awkwardly at Shaun and the Pet Finders and stalked towards the flats.

"I'll come and let you in," the young man said.

"I'm so sorry, Lance," Andi heard Stella Milton say as she followed him inside. "I thought I was early. I didn't want to disturb you before you were expecting me."

"She called him Lance!" Tristan whispered excitedly. "That must be Lance Sinden! Lance is a pretty unusual name, so the chances of there being two of them round here must be close to zero. Come on!"

They darted after Stella Milton. Andi reached the door of the block first and caught it just before it closed. She saw Stella and the young man go into one of the flats and shut the door behind them.

"It's that one," Andi said, pointing to the front door. "I wonder if we can hear what they're saying."

"Let's work this out first," Tristan said. "If you look at the facts: Lance was at the vet's with a miniature dachshund puppy on the day Koko was switched . . ."

"And Lance is related to Stella Milton, a breeder who happens to be one of Shaun and Eleanor's biggest rivals," Natalie put in.

"That's a motive, isn't it?" asked Andi.

They crept up to the door of the flat and pressed their ears to it.

"I expect you'll want to take the puppy now, Aunt Stella," Lance Sinden was saying.

"Yes, Lance, I will," came the reply. "As long as I can get him out of here without Shaun Carter seeing!"

Andi glanced excitedly at Natalie and Tristan. It looked as if they'd found Koko!

Chapter Twelve

Andi heard a tiny bark. "That sounds like Koko," she whispered, and Natalie nodded.

"I wish we could see what they were doing," Tristan said. "Do you think we should knock on the door?"

Before anyone could answer, they heard Stella say: "I'll be off then." She sounded as though she was on the other side of the front door.

"She's leaving," Andi hissed, feeling suddenly nervous about confronting the thieves who'd stolen Koko. She, Natalie and Tristan drew back a little, forming a line to stop Stella Milton getting past.

The front door opened to reveal Stella with a wriggling black-and-tan bundle in her arms.

"How could you do something like this, Stella?" Shaun demanded.

"Let me get past!" Stella protested. "I've got to take this puppy to the vet."

"I don't think so!" Shaun lifted Koko out of her hands and handed him to Andi.

Andi tipped the puppy gently on to his back. "There's the keyhole patch!" she exclaimed. "It *is* Koko!" To her relief, he looked clean and well-fed. His little tail wagged furiously against her wrist, and he batted Andi's thumb with his front paws when she turned him over again. Andi bent down and kissed his nose.

Lance Sinden came out of his flat. "What's going on? Aunt Stella, are you all right?"

"You've stolen one of my puppies, Stella," Shaun said angrily. "And I'm going to report it to the police."

"No!" Stella cried. "Please, Shaun. Don't involve the police!"

Two people came down the stairs and stopped to watch what was going on.

Lance Sinden looked stunned. "The police?" he echoed. "Look, I don't know what's going on, but you'd better come inside to sort this out."

He led them into his flat. The living room was a bright, spacious room furnished with leather armchairs and a glass-and-chrome coffee table. Stella sank into a chair, somehow managing to look frightened and indignant at the same time. Lance sat opposite her, and Andi, Natalie and Koko shared the third armchair.

Natalie stroked the puppy's head as he lay in Andi's arms, and he licked her fingers with a tiny pink tongue. Tristan sat on the floor beside them. Shaun stood, grim-faced, by the door with his arms folded.

"I think we'd all like to know what's going on," Shaun said pointedly.

Stella stared at the patterned rug on the floor. "I saw the photo of your puppies on your website, Shaun. One of them" – she nodded towards Koko – "looked just like one of my own puppies."

"We know," Andi said, thinking of the impostor.

"So I arranged to have them switched," Stella went on.

"Why?" Natalie burst out. "What's wrong with your puppy?"

"Nothing!" Stella looked shocked. "He's perfectly healthy."

"So why did you want to get rid of him?" Tristan prompted.

"I didn't. I just . . . My stud dog died of old age recently."

"Yes, I read on your website that Monty had died," Shaun said. "I'm really sorry. That must have been a blow for you, Stella."

"More than a blow! I wanted to replace him with a better dog – a dachshund with cream genes – so I could breed puppies with cream coats. Like yours, Shaun! Except there was no way I'd be able to afford one," Stella added bitterly.

"But your dogs do very well in shows," Shaun told her. "And they have good temperaments. Why do you care so much about the colour?"

"Because cream dachshunds are more valuable." Stella stood up and began to pace up and down. "When I saw on your website that a male puppy of yours, with cream genes, looked like one of mine, I knew I could switch them. I would never have shown your dog, of course, in case you recognized him. I would simply have used him to breed from. In a generation or two I could have produced a pure cream dog and the value of my litters would have soared."

"I can't believe I'm hearing this!" Shaun gasped. "You stole Koko just so you could sell puppies for more money!"

"Lance took good care of him," Stella countered. "And you've still got the same number of puppies." She shrugged. "To be honest, I'm impressed that you spotted the switch. I thought I'd given you a perfect match."

"There are lots of differences between them," Andi said. "For a start, your puppy hasn't got all of Koko's cute little habits. And there's a keyhole-shaped patch on Koko's tummy that your puppy hasn't got."

"But what about *your* puppy?" Natalie asked. "Don't you care about him?"

"Of course I do. I knew Shaun and Eleanor would make sure he went to a good home."

"How did you know when the puppies would be at the vet's for their jabs?" Tristan asked.

"It was on the website," Andi said. "I remember Eleanor telling Zan that he could check the exact date from their online diary about raising Tooey's puppies."

Lance Sinden slumped back in his chair. "I can't believe this, Aunt Stella. You told me switching the puppies was a practical joke, and your friends would see the funny side. I would never have got involved if I'd known you were planning to keep the puppy."

Stella frowned. "It would have been worth it, if we'd got away with it. I could have become the world's leading breeder of miniature dachshunds."

Andi was shocked. She knew there were some ruthless dog breeders about – Zan Kirby had been investigating them, after all – but it was clear that money was the only thing that mattered to a woman like Stella Milton.

"I want you to come back to my house and collect your puppy, Stella," said Shaun. "Then I want you to write to the Dachshund Breeders' Association and resign from the committee. You're going to tell them exactly what you've done."

Stella stared at him in horror. "I can't do that. I'll be banned from showing my dogs!"

"Good! You deserve it for what you've done to poor Koko and the other pup. And, frankly, I think I'm letting you off lightly by not reporting you to the police."

"I can't write to the committee. Dog shows are too important to me."

"It's up to you, Stella," Shaun declared sternly. "Either you write that letter or I go to the police."

"I'll write the letter." Stella glowered at Shaun, but Andi knew it was only because there was nothing else she could do. There was no way she'd want the police involved.

"I'm so sorry about all this," Lance Sinden said, as they went out of his flat. "My aunt insisted it was just a joke."

"It's all right," Shaun said. "At least we've got Koko back now."

The Pet Finders piled into his car and he drove them back to his house. Stella followed in her own car.

Andi held Koko on her lap. He'd fallen asleep with his head resting on her hand. Andi played thoughtfully with his whippy little tail. This had been one of their trickiest, twistiest cases yet!

Eleanor threw open the front door as they reversed on to the drive. "Is that Koko?" she gasped as Andi climbed out.

"Yes," Andi said, beaming at her.

"Thank goodness!"

Stella Milton pulled up on the road.

"What's Stella doing here?" Eleanor asked in surprise.

"It's a long story," Shaun warned.

In the living room, Tooey was pacing restlessly beside her basket. "It's all right, Tooey," Andi said, kneeling beside her. "Your missing baby's come home." She put the puppy carefully on the floor. Tooey gave a bark of recognition, then began to lick him frantically.

The other puppies bundled out and crowded round their brother, barking shrill greetings. The impostor puppy stayed in the basket, looking rather lonely. *He may not have the cream gene*, Andi thought, *but he's still adorable*.

Stella went over to the basket. "I suppose Horace will be happiest back with his mother," she said, picking him up gently. "Hello, little man." She smoothed his head with her hand.

Andi was relieved to see that Stella had some feelings for the puppy. And he seemed content to snuggle down in her arms.

"His name's Horace?" Natalie queried.

"It's short for 'Midshipman Horatio'. Not that it's any of your business!" Stella glared at Shaun and Eleanor. "Goodbye. I don't expect we'll be meeting again."

"I hope not," Shaun said, showing her to the door. "And don't forget about the letter, Stella. I expect to see a copy of it, so I know you've definitely written it."

"Isn't it great to see Koko back where he belongs?" Andi said, as the little puppy followed Tooey to the basket, climbed in and snuggled down beside her.

Before anyone could reply, Tristan's mobile rang. "Hi, Zan."

Andi and Natalie crowded round to listen.

"Good news," Zan said. "I've got the go-ahead for that article about the puppy switch. And the Pet Finders are going to be featured in a big way!"

"Wow! You're just in time to hear the best news – we've found Koko!" Tristan whooped.

"Well done! Perhaps we could get together for lunch at the Treetops Hotel so you can tell me all about it. I've heard they do good cakes."

"Fantastic!" Tristan said, giving Andi and Natalie a 'bs-up. "I can't wait!"

'nk you'll have to keep Stella's name out of the

article," Shaun warned, as Tristan rang off. "Otherwise the police might get involved and I promised her I'd keep them out of it."

"I bet Zan won't mind," Andi said. "His article will be even more mysterious and exciting if he has to call the puppy thief Mrs X!"

"How did you do?" Mrs Talbot asked as soon as Andi opened the front door.

"Case closed! Koko's back with his mum and dad and his brother and sisters. And Horace, the switched puppy, has gone home, too."

Her mum gave her a hug. "Andi, that's great! Well done, Pet Finders!"

"Thanks." Andi smiled. Finding Koko had been incredibly difficult – there'd been so many twists and turns, not to mention false clues that had led them in completely the wrong direction. But everything had turned out right in the end.

"OK, Bud," she said. "We've just got time for some Musical Freestyling practice before dinner." The last part of her Talented Pets project was due at the end of the week. The maths and science work was complete, and so was her poem. She'd have to ask her mum to make the video soon, so the more practice she and Buddy had the better. Hurrying into the living room, with Buddy capering round her, Andi switched on her CD.

As the music began to play, Buddy calmed down and came to stand in front of her. "Let's go!" Andi said, crooking her finger and beginning to walk forwards. Buddy backed away, keeping in time with her step. After a few paces, Andi moved her hand to the right, giving the signal for a sidestep.

As usual, Buddy moved his front feet first, then his back, instead of stepping with both at the same time.

"Never mind, Bud," Andi said. "Keep trying."

Even if he never got the hang of the step, it didn't matter. She'd always love Buddy, whether he was the best or the worst Musical Freestyler in the world. All his tiny little quirks – the way he lay across her feet when she worked on the computer, the way he sidestepped, the way he turned round before settling in the crook of her knees at night – were so memorable and lovable, that she knew *he* could never be switched.

Thank goodness! Andi thought, kneeling down to hug him.